I0741664

Dedication

To my sister, Kathy

Acknowledgement

BWL Publishing acknowledges the Government of Canada and the Canada Book Fund for its financial support in creating the Canadian Historical Mysteries collection.

Funded by the Government of Canada | Canada

BWL Publishing acknowledges the Province of Alberta for their ongoing support through the Alberta Publisher's Cultural Industry Operating Grant.

Alberta Government

Playtime

The Canadiana Paranormal Collection

Eden Monroe

Print ISBNs
Amazon print 9780228637301
Ingram Spark 9780228637318
Barnes & Noble 9780228637325
BWL Print 9780228637073

The Paranormal Canadiana Collection

2025 Releases

Night at the Legislature – Manitoba – Author Nancy M. Bell

Shúhta Dene – Northwest Territories – author Maureen Gresl

Dancing Mary – British Columbia – author Jay Lang Young

Astraphobia – Saskatchewan – author Paul Grant

Twice born – New Brunswick – author Graeme Smith

Playtime – Prince Edward Island – author Eden Monroe

2026 Releases

Ghosts of Bell Island - Newfoundland - Eileen Charbonneau and Jude Pittman

Black Gold Eye - Alberta – author JD Shipton

Haunting the Klondike - Yukon – author Joan Donaldson-Yarmey

Cardinal - Nova Scotia – author donalee Moulton

The Deepest Divide - Ontario – JC Kavanagh

Metamorphe - Quebec – author Juliet Waldron with John Wisdomkeeper (posthumously)

Table of Contents

Chapter 1

The moment playwright Jill Sayer stepped inside the house, she felt a sensation, a tingling, a sense of unease that would be difficult to articulate if she were to try to explain it. But, she argued with herself, she didn't believe in supernatural phenomena ... the paranormal. Nevertheless, she had to explore every nuance of such claims for her job of writing write a stage play on the subject, so here she was in the Yeo mansion once again. Her play would be a spoof of documented hauntings in Prince Edward Island, and a great deal of research was necessary. She smiled despite her uneasiness. She was getting too much *into her head* as Brody, her husband, often teased about her intensity while working on a project. It didn't help that she was in this big old house alone. Definitely creepy! And then she heard an otherworldly shriek coming from upstairs in one of the bedrooms...

***

"Brody!" Jill called out to her husband in the kitchen. "Can you come here for a second, honey? There's a piece on TV about that Yeo House down in Tyne Valley, the one they renovated to be part of that shipbuilding museum complex."

Brody walked into the living room, nibbling a piece of cheddar cheese. "I heard about that. They found all kinds of artifacts inside the walls, which is not unusual for those old houses. I guess they didn't have spring cleanup back in the day, so into the wall everything went. Out of sight, out of mind."

"They say the house is haunted, which is why I have to put it on my research list."

Brody settled into the recliner, listening as the broadcaster finished her story. She was pointing out that a team of paranormal investigators had visited the property and determined there was indeed preternatural activity in the restored mansion.

"I thought you didn't believe in all that stuff, Jill," he said before taking another bite of cheese.

She smiled ruefully as she muted the TV. "I don't, but I need to check it out for the play. At the very least it sounds like a fun visit. I like old places like that, and there's such a great history about this one."

"So, go and check it out so you can provide irrefutable proof that paranormal doesn't exist, is that it?" he asked good-naturedly.

"Exactly!"

"Is your play still going to be a comedy?"

"Oh yes! I like to make people laugh," she said, shutting off the television with the remote. "I think we could get some really good material at Yeo House."

"We?"

"Yes, we. You know, you and Della and I."

"You want to take a four year-old to a haunted house?"

"I wouldn't if I believed such a thing existed, which I don't. No, I thought she'd like to see Wheelie, the toy Pomeranian dog they found in the wall. The one that stands on metal wheels. She would probably feel sorry for him because he has no nose anymore … or a mouth, and one wheel is missing. I would imagine too that if they found one toy in the walls there could also be others, so there'd be lots for her to look at. I think it would be great for her to see toys that were made 150 years ago, even if they are in kind of rough shape."

Brody chewed his last mouthful of cheese, sitting back in the recliner after activating the footrest and crossing his legs. "Sure," he shrugged, "if you want to do that. It'd have to be this weekend though because I might have to work next weekend. It's so busy at the office. And while you and Della go through the house I wouldn't mind taking a look at the shipbuilding display. My great-great-grandfather was a shipbuilder over in

New Brunswick. I'd like to see the blacksmith shop too"

"It's a date then," she smiled. "I'll find out what their hours are. I can hardly wait to take a firsthand look at Yeo House."

He grinned. "Sure you don't want me to come and hold your hand?"

Jill frowned playfully. "Hardly, you have to believe in ghosts to be scared of them, so I'm going to be fine. Actually I'll also look forward to showing Della how people used to live more than a hundred years ago. It will be a good history lesson for her."

"A history lesson for a preschooler?"

"You'd be surprised at what she'd pick up. Showing her those old toys will be something she can relate to. She has asked me before what little boys and girls used to do for fun, so this will be a concept she can grasp. So win/win all the way around. You get to see how ships were built, which I must confess doesn't hold much interest for me, I'll get to soak up plenty of atmosphere for my research, and Della can see the bedrooms and toys of children from the 1800's. I guess that's what we'd call quality family time. I'm really looking forward to it now."

* * *

That night as Brody lay snoring softly beside her, Jill set aside the novel she was reading and picked up her laptop, bringing up a newspaper story about the Yeo mansion. It seemed the little toy dog, Wheelie, had captured the public's attention. He'd become somewhat of an international sensation. She studied his picture. He was actually grotesque looking, disfigured. A gaping hole was all that was left where his nose used to be, and there was no evidence of a mouth. Had the pull string for the wheeled toy been fastened somehow to his nose and had either been torn free or just fell off from constant use? On second thought the string had likely been affixed to the metal frame where he stood. In any event, those black beady eyes of his were a tad on the creepy side, but then again, she smiled to herself, how good would she look if she had spent the last hundred years or so inside a wall.

Wheelie's cream-coloured coat was threadbare in places, most of his fake fur had been loved off. It looked as though he'd provided some small child, or perhaps several children, with a good deal of fun. Had his deteriorated condition caused him to be entombed in a wall? Did the children grow tired of him, or had they simply outgrown him? It was probably the latter. Whatever the circumstance, he had not weathered his years well. She couldn't help but wonder if whoever put him in the wall had ever thought he'd become part of a fascinating time capsule someday. Had they ever imagined the little dog would see new life?

What had his name been? That would be impossible to determine of course. His new name, Wheelie, seemed appropriate enough because it was claimed he was routinely found in another part of the room from where he'd been left the night before at closing time. She didn't doubt the accuracy of the employees' account, but there had to be some logical explanation. Toy dogs didn't move around by themselves.

* * *

It was late Sunday afternoon when Jill and Brody Sayer and their daughter Della arrived at the Green Park Shipbuilding Museum & Yeo House, and by mutual agreement Brody went off to the shipbuilding display, and Jill and Della left to tour the mansion.

And there it stood on a splendid sunny afternoon, a subtle earth pigment shade of yellow ochre, with sage green trim and mid-red brick colour highlights. Now this was her kind of house, a stately country mansion that would have set the Yeos well apart from their less affluent neighbours.

"Do people live here, Mommy?" asked Della as she looked around, wide-eyed.

"They used to, many years ago," Jill explained as they stopped to look in the parlour. The polished mahogany table with cutaway linen tablecloth was set for tea, the white china cups and saucers and matching teapot in place as though waiting for guests to arrive. A settee upholstered in a rich shade of blue relaxed in the corner, amid ornate Victorian decor.

"Where are the people now?"

"This is a museum, sweetheart. It's set up so that we can see how people used to live a long time ago."

Pulling her hand free the child ducked under the stanchioned rope barrier for a closer look, but Jill quickly intercepted. "You can't go in there, Della. We can look all we want from back here, but we can't go into the room and we're not allowed to touch anything, all right?"

Della nodded her head solemnly. She was a quiet child, an old soul, and rarely had to be told twice she must not do something. Brody and Jill knew they were fortunate in that she was a very easy child to raise.

They continued to look around the downstairs, and although Jill had toured any number of historic buildings from this time period, she never ceased to be deliciously drawn in both by the artifacts and the well-prepared interpreters. She stopped to look in the pantry with its crockery and baking tins, earthenware jugs, wooden boxes and dishes all neatly displayed in authentically restored cupboards. As a writer, Jill loved to let her imagination carry her away, although this year she was limiting her experiences to supposedly haunted places. She imagined any historic property could lay claim to a ghost or two, and since that sort of thing was becoming increasingly popular, many of them did.

Up the stairs they went next, and the first bedroom they came to must have been a child's room, given the large wooden rocking horse, a handsome dapple grey, complete with a worn leather bridle and saddle. Della studied it wistfully, the look on her face clearly saying she wanted to climb aboard. Jill wasn't surprised when she asked for permission to do so, and was suitably disappointed when she was told no. A paper mâché doll in perfect condition, neatly attired in a faded cotton dress wore an expression of patient forbearance as she sat in a small wooden rocking chair by the fireplace.

Jill's attention was drawn to a toy dog on wheels. Wheelie! She stared. His face was indeed a bit fearsome. A research image was displayed in a frame nearby showing what a comparable toy of that era looked like, complete with a nose and mouth. And of course all four wheels.

"Look, Della, there's Wheelie! Remember the picture of the little toy dog I showed you?"

"He looks sad," said Della at length, her eyes fixed on the bedraggled toy. "What happened to him?"

"He was played with a lot." Jill pointed to the picture of what Wheelie had probably looked like at the time of manufacture. "See? His nose must have come off from too much pulling around. I'm guessing the child who owned him loved him very much."

Della continued to stare at the dog. "I'm careful with *my* toys, aren't I, Mommy?"

Jill smiled. "Yes you are, and it's good to take care of things, but it's true too that sometimes toys wear out. Like your Nikki doll. Remember how her hair is starting to break off because you comb it so much? That's what happens when you really love something and play with it a lot. I expect it was the same with poor old Wheelie there. He gave someone a lot of good times. Anyway, let's move on to the next room and see what other treasures they have there."

Della snatched her hand away. "I want to stay here with Wheelie."

"Okay, we can stay for a couple more minutes. You really like that little dog, don't you?"

"I do," she said leaning forward for a closer look. "I want to pet him."

Jill shook her head. "No, we're not to touch anything, remember? Everything you see in this house is really old. They call them artifacts, and if people handled them they could break. It's really special that we get to see them, but they wouldn't last very long if we handled them. Understand?"

Della nodded. "I understand, Mommy, but I'll be careful. Wheelie wants me to pet him. Can I do it just once, please?"

Jill sighed. It wasn't like Della to be so insistent, but she obviously felt a connection to the decrepit old toy. She squatted down beside her daughter. "You see that box that's around him? That's called plexiglass, and it's there to keep him safe because he's so old. That also means we can't touch him."

Della was not to be put off. "Can I touch the glass box then?"

"No, sweetie, I'm afraid we're as close as we're going to get," she told her. "Now let's move on down the hall."

Jill started away, but Della held back. "I want to stay with Wheelie."

"No, dear, come along. There isn't much time before they close this house up for the day. Let's go look at the rest of the upstairs and we can come back to this room before we leave and see Wheelie again. How does that sound?"

"I don't want to look at the rest of the upstairs. I want to stay here. I like it here."

Jill looked around at the other toys displayed in the room. Next to the rocking horse were two much smaller wooden horses, but her daughter showed them no interest whatsoever. No, she was fixated on that ugly toy dog. Not even the doll with its moulded yellow hair interested her, and Della was a little girl who loved dolls.

"No, dear, you have to come with me," Jill explained, already knowing she'd have to make a return trip on her own if she was to gather the impressions she needed in order to more fully translate this experience. But it was still fun to come with Della and see all of this from a child's perspective. She could even work Della's seeming fixation with the celebrated Wheelie into her play, anonymously, and had already begun to consider how it could be used with humour.

"No!" Della said folding her arms obstinately.

Jill looked at her daughter, surprised. The seemingly mild-mannered Della was digging in her heels over a beat-up old toy? Was this her first tantrum? At age four? She'd sailed through the terrible twos as agreeable as you please, but now it seemed the wind had shifted.

"Della!" Jill warned her in undertones. "I said we'll go look at the rest of the upstairs. There might be something you'll like in one of the other rooms. I promise we'll come back and you can say good-bye to Wheelie before we leave. Now come along."

Jill took hold of her daughter's hand, but Della pulled away stubbornly. "No, I'm not going. I want to stay here. I don't want to see the other rooms. Wheelie is here, he's not in the other rooms."

Suddenly Della dove under the rope barrier and grabbed for the plexiglass, very nearly sending it crashing onto the floor. Only quick action on Jill's part saved it. Taking advantage of the opportunity, Della snatched Wheelie from where he stood on the small table and held him to her chest.

Jill was mortified. "Della!" she scolded the child, keeping her voice low. "Put that toy back onto the stand immediately!"

Della shook her head stubbornly. As fast as lightning she darted past her mother toward the staircase. Jill caught her partway down the stairs and was able to wrench the toy from her arms. Hurrying back to the bedroom she put Wheelie down and carefully set the plexiglass over him, all the while struggling with Della who was just as determined to stop her.

Once the Wheelie exhibit had been restored, Jill picked her angry daughter up in her arms and left.

Back out in the yard Della seemed to calm down, and Brody was waiting for them when they got to the car.

"What's wrong?" he asked. "Did something happen in there?"

Jill fastened Della into her booster seat and closed the car door. "The only thing that happened in there was a tantrum, her first, and it was all over that stuffed dog they call Wheelie." She told him what had taken place.

He gawked. "You're kidding! Our Della did that?"

Jill nodded. "I still can't believe it. I've never seen her act like that before. I mean I understand that tantrums are common for children between the ages of one and four, but this was different. It felt like more, but then again I guess we don't have much experience with tantrums because Della has never taken one. I've certainly seen other children take them. Look at Marcella's Sylvester. My cousin's had her hands full with him, but Della was completely out of control in there. It was all I could do to handle her."

"She seems fine now. Look, she's playing with her doll."

Jill spread her hands. "I can't explain it, but I can tell you something for sure. I won't be bringing her back here if she's going to go crazy for Wheelie again. I on the other hand will have to come back another day because I didn't have a chance to see the entire house. I personally never want to see that toy dog again. His pictures don't do him justice. His face is ... disturbing."

Brody grinned. "Oh? Are you saying something creepy was going on in there?"

"No, other than a little girl who had a meltdown and chose a public place to do it." She glanced at her daughter who was kissing her doll. "I'm telling you, it was embarrassing."

"Thankfully it's over now. She's back to our perfect little angel."

"How was the shipbuilding exhibit and the blacksmith shop?"

"They were great. We left it much too late today but I had to get the yard work done while I had the chance. We'll come back another time, bring a picnic lunch."

Jill laughed. "Next time take Della and show her all the wonderful intricacies of shipbuilding and blacksmithing."

The rest of the day was uneventful, and on the way home Brody and Jill decided to eat at their favourite restaurant instead of firing up the barbecue as originally planned. Moxie's was a child friendly eatery that the couple frequented. Not only did it offer good downhome cooking, but Della also enjoyed the play area.

Before they had finished their meal Brody's cellphone rang and he pulled a face for Jill's benefit which she accurately read as *oh no I've been called in to work again.* Brody was a junior partner in a rapidly growing investment firm. It meant long hours and given the fast-paced nature of the business, last minute decisions to take advantage of new opportunities.

"Remember that investor we've had our eye on for quite some time?" he asked Jill. "The firm has been after this account for months. Don, one of our senior partners, got the call a few minutes ago that this guy wants to talk to all of the partners in our firm before he decides to switch his portfolio. If this thing goes through it would be very profitable for our company. It could also be another dead end because this investor is a slippery fish, but unfortunately, babe, we've got to follow up on it, and the team is assembling right now. We're going to meet at his hotel, and you know how these things go. It could last for a while."

They arrived home minutes later. That was another great thing about living on Prince Edward Island. The province was so small it didn't take long to get to most places on the Island, even travelling the direct route from one end to the other took less than four hours. He gave Jill and Della each a peck on the cheek, and then he was gone.

Jill didn't mind having the opportunity to make a few notes. Sure today had been a bit of a disappointment, but at least she'd had a chance to gather some initial impressions of the place. She was already looking forward to her next visit, a chance to study the treasure trove of period artifacts housed in the Yeo mansion.

Della had fallen asleep in the car on the way home, so that counted as a brief nap. Her naps had ended a few months ago, but given her irritable outburst today, she was in all likelihood overtired. In any event, she'd been playing quietly in her room for the past few minutes. Jill glanced at the time on her screen, then saved the file before closing the laptop. She'd put Della to bed, then come back and do a little more work before she called it a night herself.

She knew from experience that Brody's marathon meetings could last until the wee small hours, and she had no intention of waiting up. He was a big boy, he could find his way home without her worrying.

"Hi, sweetie," Jill greeted her daughter who was busy playing mommy to her huge family of dolls, "you've got to start getting ready for bed."

Della shrugged good-naturedly. "All right, Mommy. I was putting Elizabeth and Elizabeth to bed. They were tired."

Jill smiled. Della had the curious habit of giving more than one of her dolls the same name. Let's see. There were two Elizabeths, two Amys, three Sarahs, and one very special TeeTee. All the power to her if she could keep them straight.

Della changed into her cotton two-piece pajamas, her pride at being able to dress herself evident in her broad smile.

"Which doll do you want to sleep with tonight? Miss Ezzy?" Jill asked, holding up the stuffed doll with the big blue eyes. "I think she'd enjoy that."

"Yes! Miss Ezzy!" Della agreed reaching for her and squeezing her tightly against her chest. "I love her."

Once the two were snuggled down together Jill read a bedtime story before kissing both Della and Miss Ezzy goodnight and turning out the light. Della usually drifted off quickly.

Back in the living room Jill settled onto the sofa again and flipped open her laptop. Once into the file she scrolled down to where she'd left off and returned to her impressions of Yeo House. She wasn't sure how much time had gone by when she had the feeling she was being watched. Chills danced down her spine. She looked around the room, nothing. She nearly jumped out of her skin when she felt the touch on her shoulder.

Chapter 2

Jill whirled around to see who was behind her and there stood Della. She hadn't heard her walk up the hall in back of the sofa, but then again she had been engrossed in her work.

Setting the laptop aside she reached out to her daughter to come around to the front of the sofa. "What's wrong, sweetie? Did you have a bad dream?"

Della remained where she was, transfixed, her eyes staring straight ahead. The look on her face gave Jill goosebumps. The child was obviously still in the middle of a dream. It had to be another of her night terrors, although it had been quite some time since she'd experienced her last one. Usually she screamed or cried, but this was far worse. It was as though she was in a trance, and it was not recommended to attempt to wake her.

Jill hurried around to the back of the sofa in the hallway, scooped the little girl up in her arms and sat down in the recliner, rocking her gently. Night terrors were a sleep disorder and although they'd had her assessed, the specialist told them it was far harder on a parent to see their child going through something like this, than it actually was on the child. It was true, because it was heartbreaking to watch their little girl suffer like that and not be able to do anything to help. Hers was not considered to be a severe case given that they only occurred occasionally, and they were assured she would eventually outgrow them.

Della remained silent in her arms, her eyes open. Clinically she was still asleep, and would remember none of this later.

It startled her when Della sat up abruptly and leaned back so she could see her mother's face. "Mommy, why did you take my toy away today? That was mean."

Jill's eyes widened. "Your toy, dear? You still have all your toys, they're right where you left them in your room."

Della's bright blue eyes were heavy-lidded. "That little dog. You called him Wheelie, but can I tell you a secret?"

Jill nodded. "Certainly you can, honey. What do you want to tell me?"

"I can't call him Wheelie anymore because his real name is Punch — Punch Willigan, and he's sad."

That toy dog again! It gave her the willies how Della had taken to it in such a big way, so much so that she was now having nightmares about him. She couldn't blame her because he *was* awful looking although Della didn't seem at all put off by his appearance.

"Punch is sad, is he?" asked Jill as she stroked Della's hair. "You have to remember that Whee... Punch is very old and he doesn't look as good as he once did."

"That's not why he's sad."

"Why is he sad?"

"He's sad because he has to stand under a box all day. He doesn't want to do that, he wants to play."

"Perhaps they'll let him out and he can have some fun, then he won't be unhappy anymore. Now I want you to try to go back to sleep," Jill gently coaxed her daughter. "These thoughts you're having are just dreams and you'll forget all about them tomorrow."

Jill began to sing softly, Della's favourite lullaby, the one she'd been singing to her daughter since she was an infant and it never failed to produce results. It was thankfully no different tonight. Minutes later she could tell Della was asleep with eyes closed, but she'd continue to rock her for a while before putting her back to bed. She'd also make sure to leave their bedroom door open tonight in case there were any further sleep disruptions.

While she was sorry for the circumstance, Jill welcomed the opportunity to rock her daughter like this. It reminded her of when Della was a newborn and those frequent nighttime feedings. True there'd been an appalling lack of sleep during that time in their lives, but she wouldn't have traded the experience for anything. It only seemed like yesterday that Della was a tiny baby in her arms. It was hard to believe it had been four long years, and considering how fast that time had gone, it wouldn't be long before her child would not want to be held at all. No, she'd sit here all night if that's what was required, although she knew it was best for her daughter to wake up in her own bed.

She and Brody had begun to teach Della about independence, and the child was ripe for the lessons, insisting on doing more and more things on her own. Jill knew that was healthy, but oh she didn't want her to lose those baby ways so soon. Yet they couldn't very well stop her from growing up.

When it appeared Della had fallen into a sound sleep once again she carried her back to her room and carefully tucked her in, making sure that Miss Ezzy was snuggled in beside her.

Returning to the kitchen Jill buttered a half bagel and poured herself a glass of milk. It was after 11:00 p.m., time to go to bed and get some sleep herself. She had a busy day tomorrow. It was a big job to write a three-act play and she and the director, Jack Rinsky, had agreed on a final script by next spring after editing and revisions were complete. She'd easily sold him the concept of a paranormal comedy, and seeing as he'd already staged three of her plays, all to positive reviews, chances were he'd like this one too. She enjoyed the luxury of working on her plays fulltime, in addition to being a fulltime stay-at-home mother.

She had been a technical writer in the software industry before they'd started their family, creating content for documents designed to explain the nature of the company's products and services. She wouldn't have said it was her dream job, but she was well paid and the company had great benefits. However when at long last she'd become pregnant again after an earlier miscarriage, she decided to leave that job, with Brody's blessing, and write creatively on her own. She had previously dabbled in playwriting, so after Della was born, she'd chosen to focus on that and it was working out great. She had no yen to return to the corporate world as she found being a playwright professionally fulfilling.

"Mommy...."

Startled again Jill turned to see Della standing in the doorway to the kitchen. What was going on!

"What's wrong, sweetheart? Did you have another bad dream?"

Jill recalled the hot fudge sundae Della had for dessert at Moxie's. That was more sugar than she and Brody normally allowed her to have, and it had only been a couple of hours before bedtime. That likely wasn't helping any of this.

She shook her head decisively, her short blonde curls bouncing. "No."

"Are you thirsty?"

Again she shook her head. "No, I'm not thirsty."

Della's appetite had increased this past while as she was experiencing another growth spurt. "How about a piece of toast with peanut butter. I'll make that for you and you can go right back to bed before you get too wide awake, all right?"

"I'm not hungry."

Jill knelt down beside her. "What can I do for you, Della? Are you not feeling well?"

"I'm okay, but I want you to go and get Punch for me. He's very sad, and so am I."

Jill tilted Della's chin up. "Della, Punch is sound asleep in his little glass house. It's nice that you care about him, dear, but he's fine. He's not sad at all, he's just tired, so you don't have to be sad either. As a matter of fact I don't think he'd want you to be sad at all. He's got lots of little boys and girls coming to see him because he's so famous. He's got plenty of company. Now I want you to go back to bed. Come on, I'll lie down with you until you fall asleep. Let's go," she said as she lifted the child into her arms.

Jill didn't move from the bed until she was sure Della was asleep. Surely this time she'd stay that way because the child had to be exhausted. When she heard Brody at the back door she quietly slipped off the bed and met him in the kitchen.

"How did it go?" she asked him.

Brody picked his wife up by the waist and swung her around. "I told you not to wait up, although we finished much sooner than I thought we would. But everything went great. I would say we've almost got him in the bag. He's smart and he didn't get his millions by making snap decisions. In my opinion he's overdoing it, but it's all part of his due diligence."

"I hope it's worth all the hoops he's got you guys jumping through."

Brody took the carton of milk from the fridge and presumably because his wife was watching, decided to pour himself a glassful rather than drink straight from the carton as was his habit.

"It *is* worth it," he said after downing half the glass. "Stuff doesn't happen overnight, not in our business anyway. These guys like to play the game, get as much as they possibly can when they've probably been ready to lay down ink for quite a while. When it does happen it will be a big deal for us. We might be able to start looking for a bigger house, or even build our dream home overlooking the ocean."

Jill stepped into his embrace and laid her head comfortably on his shoulder. "I'm happy here, Brody. This was our very first house, the only home Della has ever known. It'd be hard to leave here for sentimental reasons, but sure, I haven't stopped thinking about our dream home. But you know I'd give up that dream in a heartbeat if it meant you wouldn't have to work so hard. I never want either one of us to get so ambitious we lose sight of what's really important in life. Each other. Our family."

* * *

She knew that Brody was tired, but was a little disappointed that he fell right to sleep minutes after they went to bed. They hadn't made love in weeks. The long hours he was putting in were having an affect on their love life, but she acknowledged that she was also to blame for their recent lack of intimacy. She too worked long hours. She remembered guiltily that she had ignored his overtures for sex on several occasions, promising she'd be right along after she finished a couple more pages, only to find him sound asleep when she did join him in bed an hour or so later. She'd make up for it one of these days.

She looked at the novel sitting on the bedside table which had been so easy to put down. She hadn't found it compelling enough to continue, struggling with a plot that for her wasn't holding up. Hmmm. If she went to bed earlier tomorrow night she'd give it another chance. She understood the hard work and endless hours authors put into their books, and she would think long and hard before she completely gave up on one. Some were hard to get into but completely redeemed themselves as the story unfolded. It could also be her frame of mind. It felt like there were a million thoughts tumbling and tripping over each other in her mind. She knew what she wanted to write and she'd already done a fair bit of research, but for some reason a really great start for the first act still eluded her. Other than that she felt good about her progress so far.

One thing she'd decided before she went to the Yeo mansion today was that the house, with its growing reputation for unusual incidents, would be the focal point of the play. However it was not so easy at times to turn frightening experiences into comedy. And then there'd been that episode with Della and the toy dog. She understood the importance of exposing her daughter to the Island's history, but boy had that blown up in her face. Nevertheless she was already looking forward to her return trip. She didn't necessarily need a narrated tour but it couldn't hurt. She knew what information she needed and it wasn't about artifacts or the Victorian way of life, except for those she wanted to zero in on. At the moment she was more interested in speaking with staff who might be able to shed light on recent events that had made the news — a supposed paranormal experience. She also needed more information about the history of the Yeo family, although she could ferret that out for herself.

Glancing over at her sleeping husband she felt her heart swell with love. He was not classically handsome, but he had a great, rugged profile. His nose, broken a time or two playing rugby, certainly provided that along with a strong chin and he had a sexy athletic body. But his kind eyes were what had won her heart. Brody was one of the sweetest men she'd ever met, but he was far from a pushover. She was attracted to his strong personality. He was a take charge kind of guy and she loved it.

They made a good couple, or so she'd often been told. She'd been a high school athlete who had gone to university on a track and field scholarship. But where she was blonde and blue-eyed, Brody was dark and mysterious — both of them tall. Not much wonder Della was shooting up so quickly.

* * *

A thunderstorm blew up in the night, waking Jill with a start from a dream about what else? Wheelie! She'd been trying to feed him kibble. She actually woke up laughing. Great! She could use something like that in her play if she still remembered it by morning and hopefully she would. The bedside clock read 3:15. Too early to go to her laptop, and besides, she wouldn't enjoy trying to function all day on three hours of sleep.

She expected to hear Della come into their room at any minute having been awakened by the thunder, but so far nothing.

35

The child was likely tired enough to sleep through one of the worst thunderstorms they'd experienced in a long while. It seemed to stay right overhead, one crash of thunder shaking the house. She snuggled closer to Brody who was sleeping soundly. She herself was a light sleeper, and she envied him the ability to not only fall asleep quickly, but stay that way. And then when seven o'clock rolled around every morning he was the first one out of bed, bright and chipper.

The storm continued and Jill felt every clap of thunder as though it was right in the room. It very nearly was, only an attic and roof away. By now she was wide-awake, toying with the idea of getting up after all and working on her laptop. She could grab a short nap during the day. Lying there looking around, a brilliant flash of lightning illuminated the room as bright as midday, followed seconds later by thunder. Would this storm never end?

Watching for the next lightning bolt, it came, flooding the window with light and her heart leapt into her throat, her scream reverberating throughout the room.

That woke Brody up! He bolted to an upright position, switching on the bedside lamp. "What's going on, Jill? Did you scream?"

"Yes I screamed! We're having a really bad electrical storm. The lightning made everything look as bright as day, and I saw a child's face at the window."

"Ooooh, you were dreaming, babe. That's all. Go back to sleep."

Thunder crashed overhead again. "No! I'm wide-awake and I saw a child's face at the window. It was a little boy and he had blonde hair. I'm telling you he was looking in at us. I saw him as plain as anything! I think he needs our help."

Brody jumped out of bed, hauling on his pants. "You really think you saw a child out there? In this storm?"

"Watch for the next flash of lightning. You'll see for yourself."

Mother Nature cooperated with more lightning, but there was no child's face in the window. "Come on, Jill! It had to be a dream."

"I know what I saw! I'm telling you, it was a face at the window!"

"Are you saying you think it was Della?"

"No, I tell you it was the face of a little boy, but he had light hair like Della's."

He switched on the light as he hurried out of the bedroom and down the hall, Jill close behind. Brody tiptoed into Della's room so as not to wake her and there she was, sound asleep, an angelic smile on her pretty face. He backed out quietly.

"Thank God it's not Della," Jill whispered as they walked back up the hall, "but I tell you there's a child out there, Brody."

"Get me a flashlight, I'm going outside to look," he told her as he jammed his feet into hiking boots, not bothering to lace them, and throwing on a rain jacket.

Jill quickly found the flashlight. "Do you want me to come with you?" she asked.

"No, but turn on the outside lights. That'll help."

"Be careful!"

The storm was already abating, the thunder not as close at hand and Jill watched from the windows as best she could. She couldn't see Brody or his flashlight. Five minutes passed. Five more, and she was going to go out there herself to see if he was okay. She was reaching for her rain jacket when he walked in the back door.

"Jill, I don't see anything other than a whole lot of rain. I searched all around the house and the garage — the gazebo. I even walked to the road and looked both ways, but I couldn't see anything. I think you imagined the whole thing."

Jill set the flashlight onto the counter harder than she needed to. "I did not imagine it, Brody. I know what I saw."

"Where did he go then? Sprout wings and fly away? The rain has all but stopped so I looked on the soft shoulder of the road but I didn't see any tracks. How old would you say the child was? Tell me again what you saw."

"I'd say the little boy was about four or five years old, very young and I saw his head and the top of his shoulders. It was as plain as if he was standing in front of me right this minute. I think we should call the police, Brody."

Brody was still doubting her, she could see it in his eyes. "Okay," he began, "our bedroom window is more than four feet off the ground, and the average four year-old is I'd say a little over three feet. And you said you saw the top of his shoulders, so he wouldn't be tall enough, Jill. Della is tall for a four year-old, and even she wouldn't be able to look in unless she was standing on a chair ... or a stepladder. Besides, the ground under the window is on a slope. You know, the privacy thing."

Jill let out a burst of exasperation. "I saw what I saw, Brody. He was looking right at me."

"Was he crying, laughing, what?"

"Just staring, really."

"Staring. What was he wearing?"

"Let me see. Considering the whole thing lasted only a second or two what I recall seeing him wear was wide white collars fastened in the front. Stop looking at me like that! You asked me what I saw and I'm telling you."

Brody laughed. "I think you just saw your first ghost, Mrs. Sayer. Maybe they know you don't believe in them and dropped by to teach you a lesson. That play you're writing is a spoof on ghosts. You could be making them angry."

"Very funny! It was real. If you'd seen what I saw, you wouldn't be standing there cracking jokes."

He shrugged, in remarkably good humour for a man who'd been jarred from his sleep by an ear-piercing scream, and then having to dash out into the middle of an electrical storm.

"We'll keep our eyes peeled for an exceptionally tall child dressed like a nineteenth century choirboy. Remember, there were no tracks, but I'll check on that again in the morning."

"You don't think we should call the police?"

"And tell them what? Why wouldn't he knock on the door if he needed help, and Jill, there's no way a kid the age you say he was, could look in that window. I'm over six feet tall and I'd have trouble getting a head and shoulder's look in there."

Jill folded her arms across her chest stubbornly. "What are you trying to say?"

"I think you have ghosts on the brain. You're doing all kinds of research so that's what you're thinking about. Our eyes can play tricks on us sometimes. Now, can I go back to bed and try to get some more sleep? I've got a meeting first thing in the morning that I can't miss. Matter of fact, I'll ask that if you do see a face in the window again, keep it to yourself and tell me all about it in the morning. Okay?"

She rolled her eyes, but couldn't help smiling. "As they say, nothing is ever lost on a writer, so you can be sure I'll use this experience in the play."

* * *

The beeping of the alarm woke them the next morning. Jill was sure she wouldn't be able to sleep after the events of the night, but like Brody, she'd apparently gotten another three hours in. It had been nearly four when they'd gone back to bed.

She felt groggy, there was no getting around that, but true to form, Brody was out of bed and headed for the shower before she even put her feet on the floor. He even sang in the shower. If he could bottle and sell that early-morning energy and cheerfulness, he'd make a fortune. She'd be his first customer because it took her a good hour before she even wanted to be talked to — by anyone. Padding into the kitchen she put the coffee on and got the makings of Brody's bacon and egg breakfast out on the counter. He had his mornings down to clockwork. Up at seven and out the door by 8:15.

Minutes later the first cup of coffee was ready and she added a splash of cream and one sugar before imbibing heartily. In about another five minutes she might feel a little more alive. Give or take. Her next order of business was to check on Della. She would never tire of seeing that beautiful little face sleeping peacefully, holding her doll. She was often up early, full of vim and vigour like her dad, but it was understandable that she'd sleep later this morning because she'd had a rough night.

Jill could hear the shower jet switched off as she made her way down the hall to look in on her daughter. Oh no!

She ran back up the hall, flinging open the bathroom door where Brody stood naked, towel in hand, having just stepped out of the shower.

"What's wrong now!" he demanded in response to her saucer-eyed look of horror.

"Brody! Della's gone. Her bed is empty!"

Chapter 3

"What!" he shouted, immediately alert. "She can't be gone! It hasn't been that long since we looked in on her, remember?"

"That was hours ago! She's not in her room anywhere."

He wrapped the towel around himself, his hair still dripping. "Okay, let's check everywhere in the house. There's probably no reason to panic."

He followed Jill out of the bathroom and although they conducted a thorough search, Della could not be found.

"You start looking outside, Jill. She likes to play in the gazebo so start there. I'm going to throw some clothes on and I'll be right out."

Jill flew out of the house, running to the gazebo first, but it was as empty. Brody met her in the yard and it took them only minutes to conduct a search of the property.

Brody ran for the house, emerging seconds later with the car keys. "I'm going to take a run up and down the road a couple of miles either way to see if I see anything, and you search the house again. If we both come up empty-handed we're calling the police.

The first place Jill checked out after Brody sped away was the window in Della's room, but it was secure, still locked from the inside. It had not been tampered with. Her heart hammering she looked under the bed and in the closet ... even the toy box. Della was not in the room but she did note that Miss Ezzy, the doll she'd been sleeping with last night, was missing from the bed. So she had the doll with her, wherever she'd gone. Taking a deep breath to try to calm herself, she next hurried up the hall and into the living room, needlessly checking under the sofa and behind the draperies. That window too was secure. Going methodically from room to room she checked windows, looked behind doors and furniture, any spaces where a small child carrying a very large doll might get into.

Lastly she went through the basement, but again no Della. If she was in this house, she certainly couldn't find her. Her throat hurting from shouting her daughter's name, Jill reached the back door just as Brody came in, his face ashen.

"I take it you didn't find anything either," he said. "When exactly did we check on her last night? It was during the storm wasn't it? I was still half asleep."

"Right around three o'clock and she was sound asleep. Oh God, Brody. I'm scared. I'm calling the police."

An officer was at their door within minutes, suggesting they search the house again, to be sure. "Those little tykes can get into some pretty small places," he suggested with a smile. "I know mine can."

"We've already gone over the entire property, inside and out," Brody told him impatiently. "She's not here."

"Was she angry at you for some reason? Was she being punished?"

Jill shook her head. "No, not at all. As my husband said we checked on her around three o'clock this morning and she was sound asleep in her bed."

"Does she have a habit of wandering?"

Jill's frustration was threatening to boil over. "No. One of us always checks on our daughter during the night, and last night we were afraid the storm might have wakened her, or my scream."

She instantly regretted those last words, guessing accurately that he would seize upon them.

She was right, his interest immediately piqued. His eyes slid momentarily in Brody's direction making it clear what he was thinking. "Scream?"

Brody shook his head impatiently. "My wife thought she saw a face at the window — a small child or something. It was likely a nightmare. Look, our daughter is missing. Can we please focus on that?"

The officer studied Brody before shifting his attention back to Jill. "Do you have nightmares often, Mrs. Sayer?"

"Not often," she hedged. This was going entirely in the wrong direction. "Can you please help us look for our little girl?"

The officer's expression didn't change. Did he think they'd done something to harm Della themselves? She supposed they had to investigate every possibility.

"Show me her room," the police officer said.

They took him there and he surveyed it slowly before checking the window for any signs of forced entry. He also looked behind the door, in the closet, under the bed, all the usual hiding places. Jill didn't care if he climbed onto the roof as long as he found Della.

Making notes, he then determined if the Sayers had any enemies. Had anyone threatened them? Had there been any suspicious activity around the house lately, the face in the window notwithstanding. No.

It was obvious that Brody was quickly nearing the end of his patience. "Can you not issue an Amber Alert? We're wasting precious time here. She'll be off the island while you stand here asking questions. No offence, but I expected more concern on your part. My daughter is only four years old."

"Officers are already looking for her, have been since the call came in," he told them. "The bridge authority has been notified. I understand your fear because I'm a parent myself, but it's necessary to gather every bit of information, determine whether there are reasonable grounds to suspect she's been abducted."

Just then someone began speaking to the officer through the speaker mic attached to his uniform. He quickly excused himself and stepped out into the hall. In a few seconds he was back, smiling broadly. "We have your daughter, Mr. and Mrs. Sayer."

Jill shrieked, quickly covering her mouth, Brody pulling her into an exuberant embrace.

Brody found his voice first as he turned to the police officer. "I'm sorry I went off on you like that," he apologized. "Where on earth was she?"

"One of our officers spotted her walking along a dirt road through a field. She was carrying a doll with her. From what I understand the female officer had quite a time getting her into the car. She was very determined to keep going. She said she was on her way to see someone called Punch. Anyway, she'll have your daughter back home here in a few minutes, safe and sound."

Della was returned to her grateful parents in under five minutes, not the least bothered it seemed by her impromptu adventure. Still in her pajamas but wearing sneakers, she had Miss Ezzy in a firm grip in one hand. Unrepentant, she was oblivious to the fact that she had done a very dangerous thing. That in itself was alarming as both parents had worked to instill the importance of staying safe.

Jill and Brody both thanked the police wholeheartedly before they left.

Brody had not even begun to relax when he squatted down beside his little girl. "Della," he said affecting calm, "it was very wrong of you to go off by yourself like that. Why did you do it?"

Della shrugged nonchalantly. "I wanted to see Punch."

Brody shifted his attention to his wife, completely adrift. "Okay, who's Punch?"

Della looked up at her mother. "Mommy knows, don't you, Mommy."

"Who's Punch?" Brody asked again.

Jill sighed. "He's the little dog I told you about yesterday. You know, at Yeo House."

He nodded slowly. "Oh *that* little dog," he said. "Della, it's a toy dog. If you want a toy dog Mommy will look on the internet today to see if she can find one that looks like Punch, and she'll order it for you. Okay? Now, I've got to get to work. I've got a very full day and Daddy can't be late … any later than he's already going to be."

He gathered his daughter into a gentle hug. "You be a good girl for Mommy and I don't want to hear about you running off again like you did this morning. I will be very angry with you if you do such a thing. Have some breakfast, whatever you want, and then you and Mommy can go toy shopping online. Doesn't that sound like fun?"

Della adored her father, and she smiled a smile that was reserved solely for him. "Okay, Daddy. Can I get two toys?"

He leaned back on his heels, grinning. "No, Della, one toy. Now, I want to talk to you about something. You know what a promise is, right?"

Della nodded. "It means saying you will do something."

Brody nodded. "Or saying you *won't* do something, and if you break that promise Mommy and Daddy could take away something you enjoy. A privilege, like Saturday morning cartoons. You wouldn't want that to happen, would you?"

Della's eyes widened. "No, I like Pretty Pig Princess."

"There you go," he said. "If you ever leave the house without your mother and I knowing about it, like you did this morning, you will have to give up Pretty Pig Princess for one whole Saturday. And I want you to know that I mean what I say. That goes for both your mother and me. Doesn't it," he said raising his eyes to Jill.

She readily agreed. "Absolutely! Della, what you did this morning was very naughty, and it really scared us. It is important that you obey your father and I so we can keep you safe. Do you understand that? There can never be a next time to do what you did this morning. Are we making ourselves clear?"

Della nodded, meekly. "I'm sorry. It was Miss Ezzy who told me to do it. It's her fault."

Brody dropped his gaze to hide a smile. It was typical of young children to shift the blame to someone else — something else, and poor Miss Ezzy came in for more than her fair share. Like when Della had taken scissors to her own hair, or made a disaster of her mother's make-up. It had really been Miss Ezzy behind the mischief.

Brody propped up the doll's face. "And the same goes for you, Miss Ezzy. If either one of you ever leave this house again without our permission, that's it for Pretty Pig Princess for a very long time. Do you understand?"

Della made the doll nod her head.

He next slid his hand under Della's chin to get the child's full attention. "All right then, you and Miss Ezzy be good girls today and I'll see you tonight. I love you!" He leaned forward and kissed his daughter, then at Della's insistence also kissed the doll.

After breakfast Della could barely contain her excitement, begging her mother to log onto her favourite toy website. However an hour later Della still wasn't satisfied with what they'd found. True, there were no stuffed dogs on wheels, or many toy dogs at all for that matter, but there were any number of adorable stuffed toys that any little girl would love to own. Della, however, was holding out for a dog like the one they called Wheelie.

Jill puffed out a frustrated sigh. If Wheelie wasn't so famous and obviously a drawing card for the old mansion, she'd offer to buy it from them, but that would hardly be an option.

"Della, dear," she said finally. "Wheelie ... er Punch ... lives at the Yeo mansion. He cannot leave there. That is his home. This is your home. He has to stay there, you have to stay here and that's the end of it. He's a cute little toy," she lied, remembering his grotesque face, "but that's the way it has to be. We can't have everything we want, honey. We've seen dozens of different toys here on these screens and if I were still a little girl I'd love every one of them. Now, if you've decided you don't want a new toy, that's all right too. You've already got lots of nice things to play with."

"I want a new toy, but I really liked Punch."

"I know you did, dear, but I guess you don't like any of the things we've seen here today. We're not going to force you to choose something you don't want, but I will ask you to make up your mind. Mommy has to get back to work right away."

Jill was tired. She needed a full eight hours of sleep in order to be at her best, even losing those two hours last night left her feeling groggy. She certainly didn't want to take it out on Della, but she'd also planned to make some serious headway with the play today. She couldn't rest on past accomplishments. She still had to prove herself as a playwright because she was far from being established in the theatre. As grateful as she was to have her plays staged locally, she wanted to go far beyond what the Island had to offer.

Della surprised her by sliding down off the sofa. "If I can't have Punch I don't want any of those other toys." And with that she flounced down the hall and into her room where she closed her door with a resounding thud.

'Great! Let her sulk for a while,' thought Jill. She'd just have to get over it. Della was a very resilient child, but she had her moods like anyone else. Fortunately she tended to get over them fairly quickly.

Jill looked at her watch. There was still an hour or so before lunch so she'd do a bit of digging online. She had tentatively named her play Ghosts in the House? and had already investigated the several other spots on the Island that boasted of paranormal activity. From graveyards to haunted buildings — even a lighthouse, ghosts and goblins were busy on Prince Edward Island. She chuckled. It was good for the tourist industry it seemed because hauntings were proving to be a steady draw. There was nothing quite like a good scare to keep the blood pumping. Ghost tours were becoming ever more popular and while she'd gone on a few so far for the purpose of fact-finding, she couldn't deny they also carried their fair share of entertainment value.

But for as many people as there were who enjoyed a good old-fashioned ghost story, there were just as many, like herself, who thought it was all a big load of hooey. A goblin scratching at a midnight window could be a tree branch jostled by the wind. Even a particular wind direction could produce an eerie sound to imaginative souls who heard the long-dead crying out to them from beyond the grave. No, everything had an explanation. It was only those who wanted to believe, those who were easily led or highly suggestible that gobbled this stuff up. Not her, and she felt sure her comedic spoof would be a winner. Hers would be a loud voice for the naysayers, although no doubt those who relied on the economic draw of scary stuff might not be favourably disposed to her play. Nonetheless she was enjoying this journey immensely. And then she remembered the face at the window, and there was no denying the instant chill she felt. Go ahead, Jill, explain that one she taunted herself.

She scrolled to an article on Yeo House, finding images of the parlour in the Victorian-era mansion. She'd studied the room on the way through yesterday, recalling a long wicker basket type thing on display. She'd never seen anything quite like that before and had immediately guessed it held some macabre purpose. She was right as she discovered it was known as a cooling casket. Apparently a body was kept in it for a few days before the wake began, like some gruesome picnic basket, to ensure that dear old whoever was actually dead. Now that was downright unsettling. Of course it was common knowledge that people were laid out at home back in those days, which must have been ... awful, but here was an actual artifact called a cooling casket. How many people had been laid in that thing while mourners waited to see if they were going to come back to life. Practical, yes, but still ghoulish. The thing even had straps on it, either to make sure no one fell out while it was being lifted, or to prevent an escape say in the middle of the night. Hearing Great Aunt Netty crying out for release would be horrible enough, no need to meet her in the hallway she supposed.

But that would be great for the play. Say, forget to buckle the straps and have whoever was lying in there cooling simply lift off the cover themselves just as they were about to be shifted into a more permanent resting place, like a coffin. Hilarious!

She continued to read about how the Victorians had a fear of being buried alive, hence the invention of the cooling casket. She guessed that one could never be too sure about such things. She was glad she hadn't lived back then. It was one thing to gush over Victorian Christmas card scenes of candles on Christmas trees and sleighs dashing through pristine sparkling snow. It was quite another to realize there were cooling caskets.

That was simply creepy, not ghostly, but were the long dead sitting up in heaven looking down on their former dwellings? She had often tried to picture in her mind, while touring a historic property, the people who had once lived there, carrying out their normal day-to-day activities. Now the previous occupants were all dead and strangers walked through looking at their stuff. It was morbidly fascinating in a way, and in her opinion cried out for comedic treatment. Not in a disrespectful way, but tastefully done. She was sure when she'd finished writing her play that the former residents of say Yeo House would have to smile.

"Mommy...." Della spoke from the doorway of my office. "Can we look for toys again?"

Thank heavens! That meant she was over her little snit and ready to be more agreeable. Perfect.

Jill closed out the file on her desktop and picked up her laptop. She'd get back to work again after lunch, and there was enough time before she made their noontime meal to get the toy shopping done.

"Sure, come along into the living room with me and we'll have another look. Is there something you remembered that you liked?"

Della cuddled up beside her mother. "I liked the purple one with pink hair. Purple is my favourite colour, but I like pink too. Can we find that?"

Of all the adorable animals in the world, Della *would* choose an octopus but to each their own. Their search for the purple toy with pink hair was quickly rewarded with an option that was not ridiculously over-priced.

"That one!" Della cried excitedly as she pointed to the toy. "I like that one. I'm going to name her Miss Ezzy."

Jill stifled a chuckle. "Don't you already have a Miss Ezzy?"

Della nodded. "She can be her sister."

"I see. Okay, the octopus is yours, and it says here it can be delivered tomorrow."

"Yay! I can hardly wait."

"That means there's one little ole sleep before Miss Ezzy's sister arrives. She'll probably be excited too, the Miss Ezzy you have now."

"She will be when I tell her."

Closing the laptop she pulled Della onto her lap. "Did anyone ever tell you how cute you are?"

Della cocked her head. "You and Daddy and Grandpa and Grandma."

"That's a lot of people and we all love you very much. Don't ever forget that."

She laughed, throwing her arms tightly around her mother's neck. "I love you too, and Daddy and Grandpa and Grandma. And all my dolls ... all my toys!"

"Okay and now I'm guessing you'd like to have something to eat. It's lunchtime and I don't know about you, but I'm hungry. How about grilled cheese sandwiches?"

She squeezed her mother even tighter. "Okay, Mommy. I love grilled cheese sandwiches."

Della made quick work of her lunch. Growth spurts aside, Jill was thankful for Della's robust appetite. Where some children picked at their food and had to be begged to eat, you couldn't keep Della filled. Jill thought about her own five foot eleven inch frame, and Brody was six foot two, so their little girl was on track to be very tall. She might even surpass her parents. She'd been a long baby and the doctor told them she could reach six feet by the time she had finished growing. It'd be nice if she were to show an interest in sports. Jill remembered when she was growing up herself that most people assumed she'd become a basketball player because of her height, but she'd opted for track. That was until she blew her Achilles tendon, a full tear that ended her competitive sprinting dream. She could still run, but it never felt quite the same as before the debilitating injury. Brody had been involved in several sports, but they'd allow their daughter to choose for herself when the time came, if she was even interested at all.

Della cleaned every crumb from her plate, even drank a full glass of milk. Jill could see she was tired, her eyes drooping even as she was finishing her lunch.

"How about a little nap, sweetie?" she asked.

"But I want to play," Della protested, albeit weakly. "I was going to do playschool with my dolls this afternoon."

"You can still do that after you wake up. You know, your doll family might need a rest too."

Her belly full, Della was becoming drowsier by the minute and merely nodded at her mother's suggestion. So walking back to her room she climbed onto the bed and Jill covered her over, first putting Miss Ezzy under the blanket with her. Della looped an arm around the doll and pulled her closer. She'd been inseparable from the large stuffed doll for the past couple of months. Wherever she was, Miss Ezzy wasn't very far away. Jill stood watching Della until her even breathing told her the little girl had dozed off. She'd walked more than a mile from home this morning, mistaking Bill Zander's potato field road for the way back to Yeo House.

Jill knew she would never forget the fright of finding her daughter's bed empty and the frantic search that followed. Thankfully it had ended well, but it had been a terrifying experience. The only positive that could come of it was if Della had gotten a good fright herself and therefore not be anxious to repeat it. Perhaps not though, seeing as how she'd been disappointed at not being able to reach the mansion. But small children tended to forget — become distracted and move on to something else. Hopefully the next big thing would be the purple octopus, the second Miss Ezzy.

After cleaning up from lunch, Jill returned to her office to resume researching. She still had a great deal to learn about the Yeo mansion if she was to interpret it knowledgeably.

She'd begun to scroll down the screen when she heard a noise behind her. Turning quickly, she froze when she saw Miss Ezzy standing in the doorway watching her.

Chapter 4

Brody was grateful beyond words that Della had been found alive and well, but her disappearance had made for a terrible start to the day and his challenges continued. On the drive in to work his car inexplicably stalled at a red light. In traffic. Not that there was much traffic in Summerside, but what there was all seemed to be behind him when his new car quit in the worst possible spot. At first he'd thought it was the vehicle's fuel saving component doing its job, however when he stepped on the gas the engine was still off and simply would not turn over after several attempts to restart. He tried to block out the blaring of the car horns. People wanted to get to where they were going. Now.

This was crazy. It was a brand new car! Boy, when he got to the dealership he'd give them a piece of his mind.

A man suddenly appeared at his side window and Brody quickly lowered it. "Hi, I'm an automotive service technician. I'm on my way into work, but do you need some help?"

Brody spread his hands. "Yes, I do. I have no idea why, but this thing just died on me."

"Okay, put it in neutral and I'll help you push it into that parking lot up ahead on the right. At least it'll get you out of traffic."

"That'd be great! Thanks!" Brody told him before they moved the car off into a supermarket parking lot. Traffic on the main drag then resumed its normal flow.

"I haven't seen any problems with these cars before. As a matter of fact we rarely see cars like these in our shop for repairs, especially not a new one," the technician observed as he looked the vehicle over. "We make most of our money on the domestics. They're cheaper to fix but we fix them more often. This one looks like a current foreign model."

"It is," Brody replied dryly. "It's only a few months old. I should have gone electric, but they offered me such a great deal on this I couldn't turn it down."

"There's probably not much wrong with it. Let me try to start it to see if I can hear something — if it'll start at all."

The technician climbed in behind the wheel and the engine turned over effortlessly. He switched it off and retried it twice. Both times the engine purred to life without incident.

"Whatever it was it seems fine now," he told Brody. "Could be a computer glitch or something. I think you're going to be okay now. Have a good day!"

Brody thanked him profusely before the technician drove away. He started the car, or tried to, but once again, nothing happened. It simply wouldn't turn over. Luckily the technician noticed Brody still sitting in the parking lot when he was stopped at the light up ahead and turned around at the next intersection.

"Still giving you trouble?" he asked as he loped back to the vehicle.

Brody shook his head in bewilderment. "It's the darndest thing! It won't turn over for me. It won't start and I've never had a bit of trouble with it until this morning."

Brody opened the door and climbed out. "Maybe you've got the magic touch. See if it'll start for you."

Once again the technician slipped into the driver's seat and started the vehicle with no problem. He then turned it off and counted thirty seconds before trying it again. The car fired to life as it should. He chuckled. "I don't know what to tell you. It's obviously a hit and miss thing and I imagine you've got a job you need to get to."

"I do and I'm already late for an important meeting, but I think whatever kinks there were have been worked out. But you can bet I'm going to stop at the dealership on my way home tonight and get to the bottom of this. I should be able to get more than six months optimum performance out of this thing. It's no good to me the way it is. But look, I'll keep it running and at least get to work with it. Brody reached for his wallet to give the technician something for his trouble.

The young man held up his hand to forestall the gesture. "I'm helping you out is all. I don't want your money," but Brody was insistent. Palming a fifty, he passed it to the technician saying lunch was on him and thanked him again.

It seemed the car's good nature had been restored as Brody pulled out into traffic. He headed for the lane he needed in order to make a right-hand turn and the car stalled once again, crosswise in traffic, now impeding progress across two lanes. The technician was long gone. Furious, Brody called for a tow truck only to be told there'd be a thirty-minute delay. The company his insurer used was tied up at an accident out on the highway. So foregoing his roadside coverage he called another towing company and absorbed the charges himself as he rode in the tow truck to the dealership that had sold him the car.

He also called the office and explained that he was having car problems and would be delayed.

"We've already been holding the meeting for close to an hour, Sayer. When do you think you'll be able to grace us with your presence?"

Don Sommers was an ass, but unfortunately a senior partner in the firm. He had zero personality, but stellar investment acumen and it was because of him that they had even had a crack at that last acquisition. Unfortunately it had fallen through, but PE5 Financials had grown exponentially since Sommers joined the team. Brody as one of the newest junior partners, was in no position to buck the man unless he pushed him too far.

"I'm sorry, Don, but it can't be helped," he told him, and explained the situation with his car. "As soon as I get everything straightened away here I'll grab the shuttle and be right over. It shouldn't be more than thirty minutes, tops. Again, I'm sorry to hold everyone up."

Sommers was typically unrelenting, his tone patronizing. "I've set my watch. I'll see you in exactly thirty minutes, if not before, Sayer. *Before* would be better."

Unfortunately it was a busy morning at the dealership, as he waited for his chance to speak with the service department manager. They'd already unloaded his car, but he had to take a number to actually speak with someone about it and his temper continued to simmer just below the overflow point.

Not much wonder he was on edge. He'd been at work all hours the night before with that now failed acquisition attempt. He hoped that investor wasn't toying with them, enjoying watching them jump around like dogs begging for a treat. But still the dance must be done. It was disappointing for all concerned, but on top of that he had to put up with attitude from Don Sommers. They'd already lost a couple of junior partners since Don had joined the firm, but the powers that be didn't value the human element as much as they did the bottom dollar. Every company was like that he decided.

And just when he was having a great sleep last night Jill had jolted him out of it with a scream that would wake the dead. It wasn't like her to see faces in windows. She was about as practical as they came but had stuck by what she'd seen, as impractical as it sounded. It'd likely only been a dream, although she wouldn't admit it. She was probably embarrassed.

He thought about Della again. He couldn't ever remember being as scared as he was this morning. And to think their precious little girl had been out all by herself and nearly a mile away from home when they'd found her. It was almost too much to take in. He'd rather lose his life than lose his child. Of course when he stacked it all up, losing either his wife *or* his child was almost incomprehensible. A malfunctioning car was way down on the list, and really, he'd only been waiting here for a little more than ten minutes.

Finally he got a chance to explain what had happened with his vehicle.

"We've had someone try it," Tom the service manager explained, "and they didn't seem to have any problem. But we'll put it on the hoist and take a closer look. It could be a faulty alternator, but don't worry. If there's anything wrong with it, we'll find it. It's all under warranty. Now I'll get Jeff to run you where you need to go in the shuttle. He's back now and ready to go again."

Brody arrived at work within the thirty-minute deadline, apologizing to everyone for holding them up and soon they had gotten down to business.

They met until after noontime, and it hadn't been a pleasant gathering. They'd lost three important clients over the past couple of months and now the acquisition of that mega investor had officially fallen through. When the meeting finally came to a close, Don Sommers asked Brody to remain behind in the boardroom.

Brody folded his arms and crossed his legs as he faced the older man. "Is there something wrong, Don?"

On the other side of the table Don Sommers leaned back in his chair, his expression pensive. "I'm thinking there just might be, Brody. I've been reviewing your HR file. You came to this firm highly recommended, but I wonder if you're able to maintain our high standards. We have to look at what each partner is bringing to the firm. In other words, how productively their time is being spent. What kind of effort they're putting in to accomplish the goals we've set for ourselves as an investment firm. You're falling short, Sayer. I know it and you know it."

Brody sat forward, stung. "I know no such thing. I'll put my work record up against any other junior partner in this firm any day of the week. I work long hours and I've recently brought two major clients into the fold."

"But nothing in the past month."

Brody stared at him incredulously. "These things take time, Don. You above all people should know that, and we still have to manage the portfolios already on our books. I'm always digging for more business. What's more, I have a very high retention rate. I put as much effort into keeping our present clients happy as I do identifying new ones. I thought that was the way it worked."

"Two clients."

"Yes, two very big clients. I'm sure you're aware of the size of their portfolios."

"Out of how many available possibilities?"

"I'm looking after more than two clients, Don, as you know."

"And how many more in the works can you safely say are close to calling PE5 Financials home?"

Brody folded his arms again. "When I can work fulltime as acquisitions manager again I'll be able to devote all my time to acquiring new business, instead of being pulled in two different directions as I have been over the past couple of months.”

“Will the car dealership where you spent time this morning be on your list, or was that another wasted opportunity?”

Brody looked at the older man as though he’d lost his mind. “No, Andrew MacTavish is not on my list. Yet.”

“So while you were cooling your heels there you didn’t take advantage of the opportunity to speak to the owner about his investment needs?”

Brody studied Sommers. “Why don’t you come out with what you really want to say, Don.”

Sommers adjusted his bulk in the chair’s limited space. He had to be uncomfortable. “That’s one thing that I do like about you, Sayer, and that’s your ability to get to the point. You’re clever, I’ll give you that.”

“Why don’t you admit it? It wouldn’t matter if I’d brought in that overseas client singlehandedly, you’d still find a way to make it my fault that he changed his mind at the last minute.”

“You’re very astute, but I do have to wonder if you’re the right fit for PE5 Financials.”

“I was the right fit before you came along,” Brody said, still on edge. “We all were but we’ve lost good people since you came on board, Don. You’re more interested in nitpicking than you are anything else. I’m not going to quit like the others did just to make you happy. I still have the confidence of the other partners and I feel I'm pulling my fair share of the load. Now, if you'll excuse me, I have work I need to get to. Nice talking to you, Don."

"As you like, Sayer," Sommers huffed, getting slowly to his feet. "Remember we've had this conversation. If there's a move for a change of guard, you won't have my vote."

On that sour note Don Sommers gathered his papers from the table in front of him and left the boardroom. Brody's sour stomach did not improve after the meeting. At least Don had finally shown his cards after playing cat and mouse with him for months. Not surprisingly the partners who had already left the firm had been replaced with people of Don's own choosing. A new broom sweeps clean as the old adage went. The handwriting was all but on the wall that he would be next, but until that happened he would continue to apply himself as he always had.

Brody had never looked for a free ride. He'd come up the hard way, struggled for everything he'd been able to achieve. He'd worked two jobs in addition to carrying a full caseload all through university, graduating in the top third of his class. It was at university that he'd met Jill Donovan and the two had quickly fallen in love. Unlike Jill, he had not earned a scholarship. He was an athlete, although with his workload there wasn't much time for sports, except for the sandlot variety. He loved shooting hoops on the weekend with some of the neighbourhood kids and up anytime for a pick-up game of football or rugby. No, Brody had never been a star. He was the guy who had to work his guts out to get what he wanted. He wasn't afraid of hard work, and to have that stuffed shirt, Don Sommers, tell him he wasn't good enough only ignited a fire to prove him wrong. He'd never quit anything in his life, although he probably should consider moving on before he gave that over-inflated egotist the chance to fire him.

His desk phone rang, and he could see it was the dealership.

"Hi, Brody," said Tom. "We can't find anything wrong with your vehicle. We've been all over it with a fine-toothed comb and came up empty-handed. The diagnostic scanner didn't show anything wrong with the computer system. We had our senior technician take it out for a test drive, and it worked like a charm. He took it all over Summerside, stopped and started. Turned it off and back on. He even took it for a spin out on the highway, and nothing. I can't imagine what was going on with it this morning, but it's fine now. You're good to go. You can drop by and pick it up anytime."

Brody thanked him, then asked to speak to the dealership owner and after a brief conversation, he was assured by Andrew

MacTavish that his investment needs were already being satisfactorily met.

It was one of those days. He thought yet again about Della taking off this morning. How had she managed to get out of the house without either him or Jill hearing her? He could understand how that might happen based on how soundly *he* slept, but Jill was a light sleeper. Her hearing was fine-tuned, even in sleep.

True there wasn't much early-morning traffic in their area but that child had gotten a long way from home, down some dirt road in a farmer's field all by herself. The thought of it still chilled him. Della was a smart little cookie, getting past locked doors and having presence of mind to make her escape silently, but something wasn't adding up.

And the face at the window that spooked his wife in the middle of the night. He'd dismissed it as a nightmare, but it still felt odd. And the thunderstorm. When he'd remarked to a couple of people about the severity of the storm the night before, they'd told him they hadn't heard anything. He'd been out in the downpour looking around the house, yet this morning there hadn't been a sign of a puddle anywhere. The ground was bone dry. Had there even been a storm? He checked it out on a weather site, and there was no mention of an electrical storm in the area early this morning.

Then there was this thing about his car. It seemed to work fine for everyone else, but when he'd tried to start it — nothing. It made him look like a fool. He shrugged it off and tried to get back to work. No, he wanted to talk to Jill, hear her voice. See if everything was all right at home.

She answered on the second ring.

"Hi, babe," he said. "How's everything going there? Della hasn't gone off on any more adventures has she?"

Jill laughed. "No, I guess she's decided to stay put, but we didn't get too far with the toy shopping, at least not at first. The toy she wanted, that old dog she saw at the Yeo House yesterday, was not on any of the toy screens and she didn't take too kindly to that. But after she got over her disappointment she decided on a purple octopus. It'll be delivered tomorrow and she can hardly wait. We had some lunch and she's down for a nap."

"Great. I'm going to pick up childproof locks for both the front and back doors. All that's required is a high quality deadbolt that's installed high up so it can't be reached by little hands. I'll put those on tonight so we don't have to worry about her getting out again without us knowing about it. Once was enough."

"Amen," Jill agreed. "Thank you for that, Brody. It's been on my mind all day. If you can't find one at the hardware store I can order them online."

"It's just a deadbolt so that shouldn't be too hard to come up with around here. It's already been a dilly of a day, let me tell you," and he filled her in about his experience with the car.

"It worked all right yesterday when we went down to Tyne Valley. I wonder why it would all of a sudden quit on you like that."

"I haven't got a clue," he said, "but I just finished speaking to Tom at the dealership and he tells me they can't find anything wrong with it. It should be okay now. What's for supper?"

"How about mac and cheese?"

He smiled. "Nothing is so bad about a day that it can't be made right with a good feed of mac and cheese. Make sure to put lots of bacon on the top."

"You betcha!" she said, chuckling, "because I know you go for that first. A person has to be quick to get much of the topping when you're around."

"I love you," he said, chuckling too, "and when Della wakes up give her a kiss for me. See you later."

* * *

Try as he might he could not get this head around the files he had planned to work on today. Don Sommers was really getting to him. He knew he shouldn't let him do that, but it was easier said than done. And he knew very well what was at the heart of it all, at least as far as he was concerned.

PE5 Financials had been featured in a national business magazine a few months ago. A really great piece that had garnered a lot of positive attention for their firm, describing them as a young company growing by leaps and bounds. The story had also mentioned that Don Sommers had been headhunted from a major competitor in Ontario, and it was considered to be a real coup for the small Island company.

Brody had been a hundred percent on board with the decision to go after Sommers, but he now regretted doing so because he'd come into the firm with the attitude that he was better than anyone there. It had quickly become clear that he felt he should be treated like a god by the small Maritime company. He was all together too full of himself, but the idea at the time was sustained growth and the other partners felt Sommers could be a key player in that regard. They'd even agreed to a senior partnership, an astronomical salary and sizeable bonuses in order to make that happen.

But while the writer had interviewed everyone on staff, including Don Sommers, it was Brody who'd gotten the lion's share of the ink. Don had been mentioned in passing and his nose had been out of joint ever since. For someone who saw himself as the star, it had been a substantial blow to his ego. He would never admit it, but Don was jealous of him. Too bad about him. He could sulk all he wanted, but he'd have a fight on his hands if he took it any further as he'd already threatened. Brody knew he might end up deciding to go elsewhere, but he wouldn't go quietly.

Just then there was a tap on the door and Amanda Leland stuck her head in. Amanda was one of Don's hires, and he had to admit she was good for the company. One of the most ambitious, determined people he'd ever met, she was smart *and* beautiful. Few clients could say no when Amanda moved in for the kill. She was one of their top performers, and any praise that came her way was definitely earned.

Amanda came with stellar credentials. She had earned a law degree then eschewed a legal career for the financial investment sector. She was nothing short of amazing, subsequently earning an undergraduate degree in business and was currently working toward a Masters Degree in that discipline. No, few people could top her qualifications, or successes, at such a young age. She was a lightning quick study and would be an asset to anyone who hired her.

"Got a minute, Brody? I have a question I need to have answered."

He turned in his seat and indicated the chair in front of his desk. "Absolutely. How can I help you?"

She closed the door behind her and gracefully lowered herself into the chair, sliding one leg over the other and crossing them slightly at the ankles. She smiled, relaxed and elegant, and if she'd chosen to have a career on the runway she would have shone there too. Amanda was multi-talented.

Leaning forward she rested her elbows on the desk, her silk blouse falling open just enough to reveal generous cleavage. "Are we still going to have that drink tonight, Brody?"

Chapter 5

Jill had frozen at the sight of the doll standing on its own in the doorway. And then she'd realized it had to be Della playing a prank on her mother. She was probably hiding around the corner tee-heeing this very minute, the little scamp. See? She'd told herself, an explanation for everything, although she couldn't forget how that incident had played out.

"Hi, Miss Ezzy," she said to the doll, deciding to play along. "Did you come to say hello to me? I thought you might still be taking a nap too, seeing how tired Della was after lunch. I guess you weren't so tired yourself, or are you lost? Here," she said getting up from her desk and picking up the doll, "let me take you back to bed because Della will be wondering where you are."

Jill went out into the hall, ready to be pounced upon by a giggling four year-old, but no Della. Hmmm. She must have hightailed it back to her room and was pretending to be asleep. Carrying the doll down the hall she opened the door to her daughter's room, and sure enough there was Della snuggled down under the cover. It wasn't like her to play games like this. She stood watching, ready to laugh when her little girl peeked up at her.

She waited. Nothing. She took a step closer, still expecting the child to start laughing at the joke she was playing, but the more she watched the more it became apparent that Della was actually sound asleep, her breathing deep and steady. Even as good a little actress as she was, there was no way she could pretend sleep as convincingly as this. She had not put the doll in her mother's office.

But the bedroom door had still been closed when she'd arrived a few minutes ago. How could the doll have even gotten out? More than a little unnerved, Jill placed Miss Ezzy back on the bed under the cover beside her sleeping child, careful not to disturb her. She studied the doll who returned her stare with unblinking cornflower blue eyes. She looked closer, recalling that the doll had a smiling face. Was it her imagination that Miss Ezzy now wore an anxious expression? No, it couldn't be. She'd never looked close enough before, that was all. This whole thing was completely crazy because she continued to hold fast to the belief that behind every strange occurrence in life there was a logical answer. However try as she might she could not even begin to fathom how something like this had happened. Della must have put the doll there long before she had noticed it and therefore had plenty of time to fall back to sleep for real. In truth though, she hadn't been working in her office for more than a half hour. In any event that was the rationale she was going to go with. No point wasting time on the search engine trying to understand this weird experience. It was a child's game.

And for sure she would not mention it to Brody. He'd looked at her as though she had taken leave of her senses when she'd seen the face at the window last night. That was still very much on her mind. Again, there had to be a sound explanation. In all likelihood she had been asleep and dreamt it. Weren't those lines typically a little blurred? This was all golden stuff for her play though. It was like a research gift that kept on giving and she was starting to accumulate a bundle of it. It was like visiting Yeo House had opened the floodgates and Jill was grateful. How could her play not be hilarious!

* * *

Jill found what she was looking for, news footage from a credible outlet about the hauntings at Yeo House, including first-hand accounts from not only staff but the never-ending parade of curious visitors who flocked to the site.

She could imagine how much the costumed interpreters enjoyed their time at the mansion. And evidently there was no shortage of stories about paranormal

78

encounters that took place there. Such as heavy footsteps that echoed throughout the house, someone with a very heavy step walking on the floor above. Also, the report included the claim that any number of objects had mysteriously gone missing only to reappear where least expected in some other part of the house. It seemed there were a "stunning number" of these unusual happenings. How could all these people whose stories would be completely unrelated, share the same paranormal encounters with little variance. Was it simply over-active imaginations at work, or something else? If so, what? Whatever the answer to that might be, it was great for her play.

She listened closely again to the online versions of the staff members' experiences. So now it was her job to come up with a reasonable explanation that would make her audience laugh. Let's say a carpenter working nearby on something that produced sounds like footsteps in the house. Could be. Or better yet, a guest closeted away where nobody could see him doing the footsteps thing by thumping on a wall. That might be even better — the guy peeking out and getting a kick out of watching staff members reacting to what they believed to be the footfalls of a ghost. That would get laughs for sure. The mansion staff might not be so amused by her lighthearted treatment of what they had heard, but she was writing a comedy. A playwright had the right to take poetic license, even with the paranormal. She meant no offence to those involved. As for the cupola whose door was normally stuck shut, being wide open... Okay, someone got it unstuck and decided to leave it that way so staff wouldn't have to deal with a stubborn door. Easy-peasy.

She was to write a three-act play, so she'd need plenty of material. Considering the information she'd already gathered on other paranormal activity in the province, it was still clear that Yeo House should be featured prominently.

She was lost in thought when Della screamed, and it ricocheted through her in a way that only a parent could understand. Flying out of her chair she dashed down the hall and wrenched the bedroom door open. The little girl sat on her bed sobbing.

Jill dropped onto the bed and took Della in her arms. "What's wrong, sweetheart? Did you have another bad dream?"

Della clung to her mother, crying. "Mommy, a man came and took Miss Ezzy away from me. She didn't want to go but he took her anyway and she's never coming back."

Jill rocked her daughter, trying to soothe her. "It was only a dream, sweetheart, and it's all over now. See? Miss Ezzy is right in the bed with you under the cover."

Della shook her head. "No, she's gone. I saw him take her. Miss Ezzy was crying because she didn't want to go. She wanted to stay with me."

"Honey, I put your doll in bed with you not a half hour ago." She didn't bother to tell her about Miss Ezzy's solo visit to her office. "She's got to be here somewhere. She likely fell off the bed. Here, let's look for her."

Down on all fours Jill searched under the bed, behind the door, in the closet, the toy chest — anywhere the doll might be. She next went through the entire house but the stuffed doll with the big blue eyes was nowhere to be found. Now this definitely belonged in the *woo woo* category. Where in heaven's name had that doll disappeared to? Think, Jill, think, she told herself. She considered for a moment that Della was sleepwalking, although she'd never seen any evidence of such a thing. She knew it was not uncommon in young children. Had her daughter just had her first sleepwalking experience? She'd gotten the door open this morning on her own, had she done so this afternoon too and she hadn't heard? She immediately rejected the notion. She wouldn't have missed that, and then there was the time element. There simply wouldn't have been time. She had only put Della down for her nap an hour ago, although a lot had happened in those sixty minutes.

"Okay, Della, let's put your sneakers on, we're going to go outside and get a little fresh air. Maybe Miss Ezzy is outside somewhere, however she might have gotten there."

Della folded her arms. "I told you, Mommy. A man came and took her away. She's not here, I know she's not, and I love her."

"The man was in your dreams, sweetie. He wasn't real."

"He was real and he told me he was taking my doll."

"Did he say why?"

Della moved her head slowly from side to side. "No, he said she's coming with me. She's mine now."

Fresh tears poured down Della's face. "I want, Miss Ezzy. I want my doll. Please go to the man and get her back for me. I miss her."

Jill released a sigh of frustration. This was for sure not covered in parenting one-o-one. "Come on, Della, I think it would be a good idea to go out and play. You've been cooped up in this house all afternoon. We'll go look outside in case Miss Ezzy decided to play a trick on you and hide in the gazebo."

Jill helped Della with her sneakers and they went out into the bright afternoon sunshine. The air was fragrant with the ripeness of late summer, a stiff breeze making the red and purple petunias dance in the front garden. They walked around the house but of course there was no sign of the doll. They continued on into the backyard to the play area that Brody had constructed for Della and her cousin Sylvester when he came to visit. The pair had enjoyed endless hours of amusement on the swing set.

"Come on, Della, how about I push you on the swing. Do you feel like flying high as you call it? Wouldn't that be fun?"

Della was determined to hold onto her blue mood. She wanted her doll and Jill couldn't really blame her. A child never wanted to part with a special toy. What in creation had happened to that darned doll? This one really defied logic. It had to be in the house somewhere. Della had squirreled it away while sleepwalking, and of course now she didn't remember where she'd put it. The dream about the bad man was obviously a child's reasoning as to how it had gone missing. Jill was sure it would turn up sooner or later, but until it did, Della would be a sad little girl. Of more importance to her now as a mother was making an appointment with her pediatrician to have her assessed. Something was going on with her daughter, sleep-wise. First night terrors and now possible sleepwalking, Della had to be seen again and the sooner the better.

Finally Jill succeeded in coaxing Della onto the swing and soon the little girl was laughing as she rose higher and higher, her head thrown back happily. "Higher, Mommy! Higher!"

"That's high enough, Della, you're not a bird you know. Hold on tight now," Jill told her, watching her like a hawk.

Della was a bit of a daredevil, but Jill knew the safe height a child should go on a swing set and she stayed within those limits.

Also, Brody had placed the swing set on a sand base with a depth of at least six inches. It was like being at the beach, but as with most parents, Jill and Brody were very conscientious about safety.

After losing a child three months into her first pregnancy, they had waited three long years for Della to come along. Jill remembered those challenging times, so sure every month that this was the month that everything would turn around, only to have those hopes dashed once again. The doctor had recommended they both try to relax and let nature take its course — translation: stop trying so hard. They'd both been checked and there was no medical reason why they were having such a difficult time to conceive, and then she'd finally become pregnant. If Brody could have wrapped his wife in cotton wool and gotten away with it he likely would have, but miraculously they made it through the entire pregnancy and Della was born a healthy baby of nearly eight pounds. So if they hovered a little, every parent who had gone through the same thing would understand why.

Jill heard the phone ringing but let it go to message while she spent time with her daughter, keeping Della in the air amid the little girl's squeals of pleasure. Her mind wandered back to the play and she could see ahead to what her evening would be like. She'd be on her laptop on the sofa all hours while Brody fell asleep in his recliner before heading off to bed. Thankfully she was not one of those writers who required absolute quiet in order to work. She could tune out just about anything.

She hadn't yet fully decided on the name for her play, still tossing around ideas such as A Spoof on Spooks, The Paranormal Explained, No Ghosts in the House, or Goblins for Hire. As usual she had a hard time coming up with a title she liked. She was still leaning toward Ghosts in the House? and as the play continued to take shape she was sure the best option would make itself known.

When Della decided she'd had enough of the swing, her mood was much improved now that her mind was off her missing doll. Jill could hardly wait to see where it showed up. It could be stuffed in the washer or dryer for all she knew, but it would be great to finally solve the mystery. Of much more importance was addressing Della's apparent sleep disorders.

"Can I go in the house and colour now?" Della asked her mother when she breathlessly finished her swing ride.

"Good idea, sweetie. Mommy's got to get some work done too, but first I think I have a telephone call to return. Let's go inside."

It was Jill's mother, Celia Donovan, who'd left the message and Jill quickly returned her call.

"Hi, dear. I called earlier," she told Jill unnecessarily, "but you must have been out."

"Yes, in the back yard with Della. She was on her swing set and I couldn't leave her to answer the phone."

"Understood. How is my darling granddaughter anyway?"

Since Jill was an only child, Della was her parents' only grandchild and they understandably doted on her. It was a job to keep them in check when it came to buying her gifts. Christmas was especially challenging. That first Christmas they'd arrived with twenty-five gifts — things they *couldn't resist*, and Della had only been six months old. But they were wonderful grandparents. They'd even sold their house in New Brunswick and relocated to Prince Edward Island so they could be closer to Della.

"She's fine," she told her mother. "She's colouring in her room right now, and likely playing with her dolls. You know Della, she lives for her dolls."

"I do. Are we still on for her visit? Your father and I are looking forward to having her for a few days."

"Everything's a go. She loves coming to your house, but I must warn you. She seems to be having some problems with sleeping. I told you about her night terrors, so you might have to contend with one of those episodes, and I'm not sure but I think she could be starting to sleepwalk."

"Sleepwalking is not unheard of in young children," said her mother, a retired pediatric nurse. "They usually outgrow all of that stuff eventually. Have you had her evaluated for sleepwalking?"

"I only experienced the possible sleepwalking episode this afternoon. I'll call and make the necessary appointment. So if you're okay with all of that, she's all yours. "

"Great! I'm thinking we could pick her up tomorrow, say late morning. We'll start by taking her out to lunch. You said she likes Moxie's."

"Oh she does! That would be great."

"I think the timing works too. It seems she's misplaced one of her favourite dolls and it could be an issue come bedtime. But I've ordered a new toy online and it's supposed to be delivered tomorrow, hopefully before you get here. It'd be good to have that to take with her."

Jill then explained about their door locks and Della's early-morning escapade.

"Not a problem. I'll have your dad pick up a couple of deadbolts and have them installed before she gets here. I think she's going to be a lot like you, Jill. You had a lively sense of adventure when you were her age, a real risk taker. We had our hands full as I'm sure I've told you before. So now with Della, it's simply a case of like mother, like daughter."

Jill laughed. "Guilty as charged. And what about you, Mum? You probably took your share of risks too, but I won't ask you what they were."

Celia laughed large. "That's right, don't ask and I won't have to tell any lies. Anyway, gotta run. We're having an early supper because we're expecting guests this evening. See you around eleven in the morning."

As soon as she ended the call with her mother Jill contacted the pediatrician's office but was not surprised when the call went to voicemail. So she left a message as to the nature of her call and requested an appointment. She'd be surprised if she could get Della in before fall, but at least she'd start the ball rolling.

She'd no sooner finished and was starting back to her office when the phone rang again. It was Jack Rinsky, the director from the playhouse.

"How's the play coming along," he wanted to know.

Jack didn't mince words. He often didn't bother with niceties either, just got straight to the point.

"It's coming along okay," she told him pleasantly. "Please don't tell me my deadline has changed. I've got a sneaking suspicion you're going to need it sooner."

He cleared his throat. "There is a bit of a stitch, Jill. It seems the play I'd slotted for the first of the year has fallen through. The playwright is experiencing some major health concerns and there won't be time now for him to finish writing it, not to mention casting, rehearsals and the lot. How close are you to being able to take his place? I know this is a *huge* ask and I could fill the opening with something else if I had to, but I prefer local playwrights and I wanted something new and fresh. I think your spoof would be the perfect fit. There's been a lot of attention in the media lately about paranormal activity here on the Island. I think that's the ideal backdrop for your play, so this has really turned out to be serendipitous. It feels right and I'm desperately hoping you will be in a position to take advantage of it. Am I right to hope for that?"

Jill was reeling. That meant she'd have to have the entire play on paper and ready within the next two months to allow time for casting and rehearsals. Even that was a tight turnaround time for all concerned, and of course there'd be changes after the readings got underway. Jack was right, it was a huge ask, but she'd dealt with tighter deadlines than that. She was also smart enough to know a golden opportunity when it was being laid before her. Jack also appreciated the value of timing as well as great opportunities not to be missed.

"Jack, I'm going to say yes. I will have it completed by October at the latest and ready to be cast. I'll make it happen."

"That's my girl!" he declared in full throttle delight. "Any sneak peeks?"

Jill laughed. "Not yet! I'll let you know when that's possible."

"Great. We'll talk again soon. Ciao!"

"Ciao yourself, Jack."

"Oh my gosh!" Jill squealed aloud. What had she agreed to? Now she would really have to buckle down and make some serious headway with this thing. Della's visit with her grandparents was a true blessing in disguise now and with Brody working longer hours these days, she'd have the time she needed to get a lot of writing done, uninterrupted. As Yeo House was her last stop in terms of research, she'd be making additional visits to the old mansion. It was shaping up to be a good source of ghost material.

She thought about Brody as she noticed the time. He hadn't said anything about working late tonight and he hadn't called to confirm he actually would be, so it seemed he'd be along at his usual six o'clock. If he was going to be here for six she had to prepare that mac and cheese, pronto. There wasn't much to it really. First she'd get the bacon cut and fried nice and crispy, then it was only a matter of cooking the macaroni, mixing everything together and putting it in to bake. She was glad she had suggested it, her mouth already watering in anticipation.

Then she had second thoughts. Mac and cheese was at its best right out of the oven, so it was probably a good idea to confirm when Brody planned to be home. Once she knew, she could time it accordingly.

She was not surprised when her call to his office went to message. He could be on the phone, but he'd get back to her as soon as he got her message in case something had gone wrong at home. A half hour went by and still no return call. She doubted he'd be in a meeting this time of day. She tried his number a second time, but when that too went to message she dialed the main switchboard.

"I'm sorry, he's not available," said Nell, the friendly receptionist. "Can I take a message?"

"Do you know when he *will* be available?"

"Probably not for the rest of the day," she told Jill. "He left the office a couple of hours ago."

Chapter 6

"So? What do you think?" asked Amanda. "I want your honest opinion."

Brody glanced around the spacious living room, one floor to ceiling glass wall overlooking the sparkling sapphire waters of the Northumberland Strait. The room was a study in modern sophistication, a contemporary design that also accommodated the nearby dining area. The key element of the furnishings was understated elegance in varying shades of beige and cream. The subtle, diffused lighting would be the room's one gentle touch once darkness fell, but at present it was awash in bright sunlight.

He and Jill had talked about building their dream home overlooking the ocean, but this would be a far cry from their own personal tastes. This was a very nice property, but it lacked warmth and coziness. It was as cool as the ocean of Italian Carrara marble that covered the floor. There was also a wealth of stylish chrome accents, but to him that only added to the unyielding stiffness of the décor. The sole attempt at alleviating the starkness of the room was the lone pillar candle sitting atop a polished chrome side table.

"Well?" she asked with a mock pout, not used to being kept waiting. "What do you think of my new home? I told you I was looking to buy and this one came on the market so I snapped it up."

"How many million will this set you back?" he asked, returning his attention to her.

"A couple or so," she replied, looking at him coquettishly. "My grandfather said to find what I wanted and let him know how much."

Brody tilted his head as he regarded her, perplexed. "Now that surprises me, Amanda. If anything I thought you would be your own woman. Buy your own home ... *earn* your own home."

If she took umbrage at his remark, she hid it well. "I did earn this home. The deal was made many years ago that if I was dedicated to my education and made something of myself, I would be amply rewarded. My grandfather is a centimillionaire, and all in liquid investible wealth as you know. This little shack only set him back three and a half million, and it's nice to have someplace to get in out of the rain."

He laughed. By contrast, his seven hundred thousand dollar home *was* a shack, but he far and away preferred it to this glass castle.

She looked at him more sharply. "I'm guessing it's not to your taste, but that's fine. I can sell it and we can keep looking."

"If you like it, Amanda, keep it. What does it matter what my tastes are? I already have a home."

She smiled that great smile of hers as she strolled out onto the patio, the ocean only metres away beyond the red sandstone cliffs. "I loved the privacy here right away. It's like being in our own little world," she said as she dispensed with the rest of the buttons on her silk blouse, letting it slip from her shoulders onto the floor. Clad now in only a gossamer brassiere, she turned to face him.

He drew in his breath. "Amanda..."

"Don't you appreciate the ... view, Brody? Surely you can't be the only man alive who doesn't think I'm desirable."

Reaching behind she undid the bra's clasp in one lithe movement and the silk undergarment also dropped to the floor. She faced him, topless.

Brody felt the flush that started somewhere south and quickly spread throughout his body. She *was* desirable, breathtakingly so! He'd seen a body like Amanda's once. It was a marble statue, but those rounded curves were much more appealing in the flesh. Still, he turned away.

She smiled seductively, as though certain of her power over him. Covering the distance between them she slid her arms around his neck and brought her lips against his.

She tasted like mint. He stepped away.

"Why are you playing hard to get? You're not some nervous teenager, you're a grown man who I'm sure knows his way around a woman's body."

He ran a hand over his face. "Maybe because I *am* hard to get. I'm a married man, Amanda. I'm taken. This whole thing is dead wrong."

Her smile stopped short of her eyes as she came to him again, one hand boldly assessing him. Her smile deepened. "I knew you wanted me. You've been playing with me for weeks, but I want more than a few stolen kisses. I play only for high stakes and I'm tired of waiting. I'm the best thing that's ever come into your life, admit it."

He stepped back again. "You're forgetting about my wife. She's a beautiful woman."

She shrugged dismissively. "I've seen the obligatory family portrait on your desk. She's passably pretty I suppose, and your daughter is kinda cute. That's fine for a first marriage but think how proud you'll be to have *me* on your arm."

"Come on, Amanda! That's enough."

"Sorry," she said. "I guess I struck a nerve. Anyway..." She ran her hands over her breasts, teasing him.

He knew this was wrong on every level. His entire being screamed it, but try as he might he could not look away. She had a body that invited a man's touch, her skin as smooth and lustrous as satin. It was true that this thing had been building between them for a while. Amanda Leland was the entire package, a package that any man in his right mind would grab with both hands and hang onto. She only had to crook her finger and men swooned. He'd felt it on a visceral level when she'd turned her sights on him, and immensely flattered, he had responded. She was a beautiful, deadly spider and once pounced upon, the victim pretty much knew it was all over. Usually, he told himself, but he was not anybody's victim.

"Amanda, get dressed. This isn't a good day."

She began to unbuckle the slim leather belt at her waist and once undone, the zipper began its enticing descent, until his hand arrested its progress. "I said not today."

Sparks flew from her gold-flecked eyes. "It's never a good day. What will it take to get you into bed, Brody? I'm tired of being held at arm's length. I'm over eighteen as you can well see. You don't need my daddy's permission to bed me."

"Get dressed."

"No, I plan to get *undressed*," and with that she dropped her slacks and they pooled at her feet. She stepped out of them, wearing only the briefest of underwear. Also gossamer thin, they left exactly nothing to the imagination.

A man could only stand so much, but he'd learned a long time ago to keep his mind no matter how challenging the circumstances. "Like you say, Amanda, you're over eighteen. So why are you acting like a schoolgirl? Are you actually trying to wear me down like I'm some weak-kneed college boy? I would have expected better of you. You'll have to up your game if you want to play in the big leagues my girl. It's all about power, and who do you think has the advantage right now? Not the one who's all but naked and vulnerable. Now put your clothes back on and we'll deal with this like adults, not a couple of randy teenagers who go all out because they've got the house to themselves."

She laughed derisively. "You know, that take charge attitude of yours is what attracted me to you in the beginning. I like that you know your own mind and don't take any crap. So neither will I. You're a winner, Brody Sayer, and I want to be your wife. I can't be any more upfront than that."

He folded his arms across his chest as he watched her. "I've told you, I'm not available for the taking. I already have a wife and I'm not looking to make any changes in my marital status."

She threw back her head and laughed. "Your reluctance whets my appetite. You know how competitive I am, the more you back off the more I want you. You become even more interesting to me, even more of a challenge and I adore challenges. Now, put that in your pocket and take it home with you. And," she said, disposing of her briefs and striking a tantalizing pose, "you can take a mental image of this home with you too. I guarantee it won't be easy to forget, men being so visual and all."

Amanda did get back into her clothes once she'd made her point and as promised drove him to the dealership in Summerside, arriving just as they were about to lock their doors for the night. And thankfully he was able to make it home to O'Leary without so much as a ripple in his car's performance. The drive was uneventful, the day's traffic subsided now that rush hour was long past. It was such a satisfying feeling to come home to Jill, the woman who had his heart. There was no comparison worth making with what he'd seen an hour ago. His wife would win hands down.

He met Jill in the kitchen. There was no mac and cheese in evidence and he realized as he lifted his eyes to the clock on the wall that suppertime had passed nearly two hours ago. He was starved, but hardly in a position to inquire what had happened to the evening meal. It had been a warm day on the Island, but there was a definite chill in the air here.

Della ran into the kitchen and grabbed her father's legs. "Daddy!" she squealed. "You're home!"

He scooped her effortlessly into his arms and swung her around. "Della Bella," he teased her with his play name. "What did you do today? Did you have fun?"

The next few minutes were spent with Della's detailed account of her day, as Jill slipped past wordlessly and went into her office and closed the door. She was not the jealous wife type. She would refuse to play that card, but he knew she wondered where he'd been since he hadn't told her he'd be working late. But she wouldn't dampen Della's excitement at seeing her father. She'd let them have their time together no matter how put out she was.

It was close to a half hour later when he tapped on her office door and stepped inside.

"I'm sorry about supper," he said, "and that I didn't call you back. I won't do that again. Now, I imagine you and Della already ate, did you?"

"I fed Della because she's got to go to bed in a few minutes. She had a nap this afternoon so I can let it go another half hour, but no, I didn't eat. I was kind of wondering why you didn't return my call. I needed to find out when you'd be home so I'd know when to put the mac and cheese in the oven. I wanted the casserole to be at its best for you. So why didn't you? What if it had been an emergency with Della? And please don't say you had a meeting because I spoke with the receptionist at four o'clock and she said you'd left a couple of hours before that. It's almost eight o'clock, Brody. I guess I'm most upset that you ignored my calls. The rest I'm sure you can explain."

He didn't reach for her. He knew Jill, she'd only push him away until everything that needed to be said, got said. She was very open with him about *her* time, and she deserved nothing less from him. He began by telling her about the warning of termination by Don Sommers, that it had been an all around bad day that hadn't been made any better by the debacle with the car on his way to work. He told her he'd left the office early this afternoon to go with a colleague who wanted his opinion on a recent property purchase on the outskirts of Stratford, and that colleague had driven him back to the dealership in Summerside. The whole thing had taken longer than he'd expected, but he'd come straight home from there except when he'd stopped for the deadbolts.

When he was finished Jill allowed him to pull her into a hug, but she was still distant. She was smart, no doubt picking up on his evasiveness about the colleague. He took a step back.

"I've got an idea. Why don't you put Della to bed and I'll call in a pizza. Then I'll put the deadbolts on and kiss Della goodnight before I go pick up our order. That'll give you a chance to read to her. How does that sound?"

"Sure, but no pepperoni on my half," she told him, although she was still not smiling. "And then when we're both full, we can talk because I think there's still some things that need to be said. Sound like a plan?"

His heart sank. "Sure, babe. I think I'll call that new place in town, give it a try. I know a couple of people who ate there and thought it was great. I'll order an extra-large because I'm famished and you can heat some up tomorrow for lunch. And yes, I'll get extra cheese. You're welcome," but even adding that last remark didn't succeed in breaking the ice.

When he got to the pizza shop he was surprised to see a tour bus in the parking lot and the restaurant full. Who'd have thought there'd be a rush at this time of night? His order had likely preceded the bus crowd, so there'd be no wait. Wrong. There was only two teens on duty and while they were doing a great job, they were clearly overwhelmed. The girl waiting the counter had not been hired for her interpersonal skills, and she told him his pizza would be along in ten or fifteen minutes. No problem. He'd have preferred to have it ready when it had been promised, but that was life. You had to go with the flow. That commitment had obviously been made before the bus crowd arrived.

So he went back to his car and fifteen minutes later on the dot, presented himself at the counter again only to be told it'd be ready in another ten minutes "for sure". Close to an hour later he left with the pizza, but the delicious aroma promised to make up for the delay.

He found Jill in her office. "Sorry for the wait, they were crazy busy as it turns out. Do you want to eat in the kitchen, or in front of the TV?"

She saved and closed the document she'd been working on. "I was beginning to wonder if you were coming back at all," she told him solemnly as she headed for the kitchen.

"Why on earth wouldn't I come back?" he asked as he followed her and opened the box, waiting for her to put out plates and fetch them each a beverage.

"Why indeed," was all she said before she changed the subject, bringing him up to date about Della's possible sleepwalking and the missing doll.

She swallowed a mouthful of pizza before she continued. "I was really dreading bedtime because I thought I'd have trouble settling her down without her favourite doll."

"She has lots of dolls."

"True, but she's fixated on that one. Miss Ezzy she calls her and there was quite a hullaballoo this afternoon when she went missing, but that's another story. I was thinking how I could get around it when I walked into her bedroom tonight and there was that very doll sitting on her bed. I was stunned. I mean I turned this house upside down and the doll is big so it's not like it could be easily overlooked."

Brody was chowing down on a slice of pizza. "What do you make of that?" he asked around a mouthful.

Jill shrugged. "Like I said I think Della may be doing a little sleepwalking. I should hear back from her pediatrician tomorrow as to when he can see her and begin the process of having her assessed. It has to be pursued."

"Of course!"

"But the doll is back, wherever it may have been, and right now that's all I care about. I remember my mother saying when I was a kid I had a little toy rabbit that I carried with me everywhere. It was a ragged old thing at the end of it. Mum said she washed it so many times it was literally falling apart. And then one day it vanished, and we never did find it. My mother said I could not be consoled. I cried for hours. They replaced it as best they could, but I never took to the new bunny. That's why I was dreading facing bedtime tonight without Miss Ezzy. I was glad we'd ordered a new Miss Ezzy, only this time it's that purple octopus I told you about."

Brody laughed. "Yeah, a purple octopus, but she gave it the same name as the doll. Now there'll be two Miss Ezzy's."

Jill chuckled. "Several of her dolls have the same names, but she says they all understand which one they are."

"I'd say with her imagination, she's going to end up being a writer like her mother. What do you say about that?"

"Time will tell, but right now it's all about her dolls. At least she'll have Miss Ezzy when she goes to Mum and Dad's tomorrow. If you recall, they're coming to take her for a few days. I think the new toy she ordered will be here before they come in late morning, so my parents had better have lots of room in their car for the entire menagerie."

Brody sat back, letting the three slices he'd wolfed down, settle. "I'm glad she enjoys being a kid. She'll outgrow those toys soon enough. It seems like yesterday she was born and now here it is four years later."

Jill nodded wistfully. "And now I have to ask you, Brody, will you and I have another four years together?"

He looked at her sharply. "What kind of question is that! Of course we will."

Jill sighed as she pushed her slice of pizza aside, barely touched. "Call it a gut feeling, call it women's intuition, but I'm guessing there's another woman in your life these days. Am I right or am I wrong?"

"Jill..."

She held up her hand. "I said I wanted to talk, and this is that talk. I think it's a fair question and as your wife I'm entitled to have it answered. Is there, or not? The answer is either yes or no."

He suddenly felt as though he had swallowed a bowling ball, the pizza threatening to turn on him. Jill had a way of cutting to the heart of a matter better than anyone he knew. He knew he felt that way because what she said mattered more to him than anyone else's opinion ever could. He searched for the right words.

"It's a yes or no question, Brody. I'm going to guess that because of your hesitation the answer is yes, am I right? Are you seeing another woman?"

Brody stared at her, the gulf between them widening by the second. Never had he loved his wife more than at this very moment, now that everything he cherished was on the line.

He ran his hand over his face, suddenly exhausted. He had an idea in that moment what it would be like to face a firing squad. It was not a simple yes or no answer, well yes it was, but he couldn't just let the answer dangle there with no immediate explanation. It would be the words that followed the admission that would make the difference. The truly terrifying part was whether or not Jill would listen.

He cleared his throat. "Jill..."

"Yes or no, dammit! Yes or no!"

"Ease up! I feel like I'm on trial for my life."

Her eyes had become ice blue granite. "Maybe that's because you are, and the life that's on the line is yours and mine ... together. At least have the courtesy to give me an honest answer."

Brody's heart was beating double time. "Even if I said no, you wouldn't believe me because I think you already have your mind made up."

"I do have an idea what you're about to tell me, but I want with every fibre of my being to be wrong. That you love only me and would never even look at another woman, but I'm not about to hear that am I, Brody?"

"What, that I don't love you?"

"If ever I saw a drowning man grabbing for a life ring that keeps floating out of reach, it's you. I say again, the very least you owe me is honesty, as you have every right to demand the same from me. To me, our marriage vows are sacred. I would not even look at another man."

Brody threw up his hands. "Come on, Jill. I've seen you looking. Everyone looks, it's crossing the line that's wrong."

She adjusted herself in the wooden chair. "Alright then, have you crossed that line? I don't know why I'm even bothering to ask, it's written all over your face. Tell me!"

"I'm trying! Give me a chance, dammit!"

He leaned his head back against the wall. How many times in the past few weeks had he played this very scenario out in his head, having to explain himself to his wife. That was always the risk in anything like this, being somehow found out. He felt like the worst husband alive at the moment.

"Jill, it's not what you think."

Della walked into the kitchen, dragging a toy.

Great! Now they'd gone and woke Della up. This poor kid with her sleep issues and Mommy and Daddy arguing had probably deprived her of a good night's sleep.

The little girl looked at her father, her eyes troubled. "Are you and Mommy fighting?" she asked, her bottom lip trembling.

Jill started for her but Della backed up. She too wanted an answer, and he was the one sitting squarely on the hot seat.

He kept his tone gentle. "It's all right, Della. Mommy and I are having a … discussion. That's all. Everything's all right, now go on back to bed. Would you like me to take you down and tuck you in?"

Della shook her head. "No."

Brody pointed to Jill, whose expression had softened in favour of the child. "What about Mommy? Would you like her to tuck you in, read you another story?"

That earned him a surreptitious glare from Jill.

Once again Della shook her head. "No. I want you to stop yelling at each other. It makes me sad."

Brody closed his eyes. He and Jill had about as peaceable a relationship as was possible. They rarely argued, and almost never raised their voices at one another. Apparently one bad night sank the ship.

"Della, mommies and daddies raise their voices at each other sometimes," he explained. "It doesn't mean anything bad is going to happen. Your mother and I love each other very much, and we both love you. Now, there's nothing to be concerned about, all right?"

The child nodded, although still sombre. "Give Mommy a kiss," she suggested, "like you used to."

Now there was a damning indictment. *Like you used to*. Out of the mouths of babes... Had they really begun to drift that badly? "I will, honey," he assured her, "now you go back to bed."

He looked to see what Della was dragging behind her, but it was Jill who asked.

"What have you got there, sweetie? It looks like your little chalkboard."

Della smiled. "It is and Miss Ezzy showed me what to put. Do you want to see?"

Brody and Jill both readily agreed.

Della turned the chalkboard around and held it up. There printed in bold pink chalk letters was: DADDY LOVES AMANDA

Chapter 7

Brody froze, watching as the colour drained from Jill's face. He'd never seen her so pale, and there stood a smiling Della in the doorway holding up the chalkboard with its incriminating declaration.

"I can read it too," she announced. Pointing to each word she read aloud: Daddy loves, I don't know what the last word is. I never printed it before, but Miss Ezzy knows. What does it say, Daddy?"

Jill stepped in for the save. "It's just a name, dear, and you did really good to print all that. Now come along back to bed," she said taking the chalkboard from Della and leading the little girl by the hand down the hall to her bedroom.

It seemed like forever before she returned, Brody wondering at one point if she even planned to. He was still stunned. How had Amanda's name ended up on that chalkboard? Della didn't even know the word she'd apparently printed, and some doll had told her to do it? Yeah, a doll named Jill, although he immediately cast that thought aside. How would anyone know Amanda's name in the first place, unless the receptionist had told his wife he'd left the office today with Amanda Leland. That had to be it. But still, he'd never known Jill to play that kind of game. It was beneath her. But what other explanation was there?

Finally Jill came back to the kitchen where he sat beside the open box of pizza. He should have taken the time to put the leftovers away, but he felt as though he was rooted to the spot.

She didn't say a word as she got a container from the cupboard, placed the leftover pizza slices in it and set it in the fridge. And then she turned to face him. "Brody, I want you to sleep in the spare room tonight. As I've told you, Della is leaving before noon tomorrow to go with my parents for a few days. I suggest we wait until after she leaves to have a conversation about this."

A million feelings raced through his mind, chief among them regret for the pain he saw on his wife's face. Jill was not a crier unless she had a very good reason, although she did look as though she was about to break down at any moment. He was a fool, that part was not up for discussion, but for some unearthly reason he was angry with her about the chalkboard.

"I agree," he said quietly. "I have obviously screwed up..."

"Big time."

"Yes, I admit it, big time. But was it necessary to involve our daughter? She's only four years old, Jill."

She wheeled on him. "Involve her in what way?" she demanded, her voice a hoarse whisper.

"Were you aware of what was printed on that chalkboard? Did the receptionist tell you her name today?"

"Don't you dare try to turn this around," she hissed at him. "Seeing that name was as much a shock for me, as it was for you to be found out in such a way. If I didn't feel as though my life was basically over at this moment, or in the very least my marriage, I'd have gotten a laugh out of the look on your face. If ever someone was served their just desserts, buddy, it was you here tonight. I guess I don't have to wonder who my rival is. Her name is Amanda. Am I right?"

"Jill, come on..." Brody reached out, but she pushed his hand away.

"Do not touch me!" she warned him in undertones. "At least show me that much respect. Now, we can't get into this mess tonight without raising our voices, I know I can't, but let me say this. There's a price to be paid for playing around, Brody, and playtime can turn out to be very expensive. I will not allow you to continue to make a fool out of me."

And with that she left the kitchen and went into the master bedroom, resisting the urge to slam the door. Jill was a door slammer of the first order, but common sense prevailed. They both had their daughter to think about.

Jill barely made it to the master bath before the pizza she'd managed to get down reversed direction. And that's when she allowed the tears to come, and they came in a flood. She gave them full vent, stifling her sobs. Della had ears like a radar receiving system and she couldn't risk her daughter overhearing her. She and Brody were going to have the perfect opportunity to talk tomorrow after Della left, but what then? Could they work through this? Was that even a possibility? She'd often wondered what she'd do if she was ever faced with such a situation, like her good friend Paula had been. Paula had decided to forgive her husband of ten years despite his three-year affair with a co-worker. And they did seem to have recaptured their love for each other, but how could she ever trust him again? How was that even possible?

She knew what Brody's reaction would be if it were his wife who had strayed. He would not handle it well. She thought about their wedding day, how Brody had been moved to tears when he'd watched her walk down the aisle to him, pledging "with all my heart" to love her and honour her. And now eight short years later here she sat on the bathroom floor, sick to her stomach and crying her eyes out over his infidelity. The next question was how long it had been going on. Months? Years? What would Brody have to say for himself? What *could* he possibly have to say for himself now that the cat had been let out of the bag.

She'd thought just last night how it'd been much too long since they'd made love, but then he had been working such long hours. Attending a lot of high-pressure meetings, or so he'd said, with the company's growth depending on a positive outcome. She hadn't pressed him about it. She also knew some of the blame was hers, although she had initiated sex one night and been told he was too tired, too preoccupied. Too preoccupied alright! Of all the men she'd guess might play around on their wife, her husband hadn't made the list. And what about that horrible message on the chalkboard? She'd erased it when she'd taken Della back to her room, but how had it ever gotten there in the first place? The whole thing didn't make any kind of sense.

She then thought about the commitment she'd made to Jack earlier today to have the play written and ready to be cast in two months. How on earth could she concentrate on that now with the bottom having fallen out of her world? But then on second thought it might prove to be providential if it took her mind off this because at present everything felt completely upside down. She desperately loved her husband, but where had it gotten her? *Cheated on, that's where* she told herself brutally as she sat on the floor with her back against the tub. She'd heard about the seven-year itch for couples, something she would have laughed off mere hours ago. Did anyone ever really know another? Apparently not. And while Brody had not come right out and said he was involved with another woman, he had not denied it either which he would have, vehemently, if he wasn't playing around on her.

Sometime in the early morning hours she picked herself up off the floor and walked slowly to Della's room to check on her. She was sleeping peacefully. Making her way back to the master bedroom she didn't even bother to undress as she pulled back the quilted spread and slid in under it. She didn't think sleep could possibly come, but when she woke thick headed the next morning she realized it must have. She could see grey skies from the bedroom window. How appropriate.

A quiet knock sounded at the bedroom door. She glanced at the alarm clock. Six-thirty. It had to be Della, or was it Brody? Her heart betrayed her with a leap at the thought of him, as it always did, but she thrust it away.

"Come in," she called out softly, and Della padded into the room carrying Miss Ezzy.

Without invitation the little girl climbed onto the bed and nestled down under the cover beside her mother.

"Daddy's gone," she said, and if it was possible for Jill's heart to fall any further, it just did.

Had he even spent the night in the spare room at all? Yes, he had, she quickly remembered. She'd heard him snoring when she'd passed by to check on Della. *He* didn't seem to be at a loss for sleep.

"He had to leave early for work this morning, honey."

"But he didn't even say goodbye and I'm going away today."

"He's got some things he has to do and he asked me to give you a kiss goodbye for him," she finished, cringing at the outright lie.

"Why are you and Daddy so sad?"

Jill sighed. Good luck trying to hide anything from a child. And how would Della fare in all of this if she and Brody did break up? She was thinking about how she could find it in her heart to forgive her husband, but really, did he care if he was forgiven or not. Had he already chosen *Amanda* over her and would ask for a divorce? Maybe there was no need to weigh options about whether or not to continue her marriage because there might not be any.

Tears threatened again, but she forced them away.

"Do you want to try to go back to sleep, sweetie? Grandma and Grandpa won't be here for another few hours, so there's plenty of time to have breakfast and get ready."

"Isn't my toy coming today?"

She found it in herself to chuckle. "You're right, it is supposed to arrive today. Let's hope it comes before you have to leave. You're going to have a lot of fun on your visit with Grandma and Grandpa. They're going to take you somewhere special for lunch, a place I know you'll really enjoy."

"Yay! Is it where we went before?"

Memories of their recent family outing washed over her. It felt now as though that had happened in the distant past. Della was overjoyed when Jill told her it was the same restaurant.

Jill felt sleep tugging at her and she put her arm around her daughter and snuggled closer to her. The two were soon fast asleep. It was after eight o'clock when Jill looked at the clock again. This time she had to get up and face the day, attain some semblance of normality or else her mother would be asking questions. The last thing she wanted to do was discuss her marital problems with her parents. Her father and Brody got along great ... now ... but to her dad she was still his little girl and would roar to her defense. No, she'd keep everything to herself until she and Brody discussed the matter and she had a chance to make some sense of everything.

Della was awake now too, so feeling as though she'd slept on the side of the road and likely looking as though she had, Jill got up and made breakfast for her daughter, grabbed a quick shower and began to pack

Della's suitcase. Of course she wanted to take practically every toy she owned with her, but she was finally persuaded to choose two dolls, her colouring book and crayons and a few books so Grandma could read her favourite stories to her at bedtime.

"Can I take my chalkboard with me too?" Della begged. "There's words on it again."

The chalkboard was still standing in the corner where she'd placed it last night after putting Della back to bed.

"Have you been writing on it again, Della?"

The little girl shook her head. "No."

"Then how do you know there's anything on it?"

"Miss Ezzy told me."

"And what did Miss Ezzy tell you is on the board?"

"She said you have to go and look."

Jill's stomach began to churn. Her reasonable explanation theory had sorely been tested over the past two days and now she stood gazing at the back of the chalkboard, actually frightened to turn it around. Her feet were suddenly made of stone, preventing her from walking the few feet to the board and seeing what was on it.

Della hopped down off the bed. "I'll go and see what it is, Mommy."

"No!"

Startled, Della jumped back and began to cry.

Jill knelt down and pulled her daughter into a hug. "I'm sorry, Della. I didn't mean to shout like that. Mommy's not feeling the best today. Alright, you go and get the chalkboard, honey, and see what the message is."

The tears didn't last long and as Della wiped her eyes, all smiles again, she retrieved the chalkboard and brought it back to her mother. The message was printed in yellow chalk : EZZY LOVE DELLA

Given the messy scrawl it seemed Della had printed it herself, and Jill's relief was palpable. She had taught Della how to spell Miss Ezzy's name, and she certainly knew how to print her own name. The "S" had even been left off LOVE. Yes, a four year-old had definitely printed this message.

"That's a wonderful thing for Miss Ezzy to say," she told the little girl, kissing her forehead.

The phone rang in the kitchen and Jill left Della alone to play while she ran to answer it. Glancing at the caller ID, she saw it was Brody.

"Hello," she said, without warmth.

"What time would you like me back home?" he asked. "We should finish our weekly finance meeting around noontime and I could take an extended lunch break."

This time yesterday she couldn't have imagined she'd be making an appointment with her husband to talk about whether or not their marriage could be saved.

"Fine, Della should be gone by eleven so that would work out. Come during your lunch break, but I warn you it's not going to be a pleasant conversation."

"I never said I thought it would be."

"Good. Be prepared for unpleasant. I hate you for putting us in this position. I am absolutely furious with you."

There was a long pause on the other end of the line. "It's what I expected."

"It's what you deserve."

"Touché! But there are things that have to get said, Jill, and I'm pretty sure you won't want to hear some of them."

"I don't want to hear any of them if you want the truth, but this isn't a time for sticking our heads in the sand. And since you've found someone better, then that'll be your opportunity to tell me all about her. Brag about your good fortune."

"Stop it, Jill! Just stop it. I'm not going to get into all of this right now."

She took a deep breath. "You're right. I'll see you when you get home."

"Jill... Oh never mind. I'll see you later."

A cup of coffee. That's what she needed to clear the remaining cobwebs from her brain. If she hoped to fake any kind of normality when her parents arrived, she needed to get with the program, and fast. She had no appetite for breakfast, even watching Della eat her cereal made her want to gag. But she could keep a cup of coffee down. Black. A jolt of much-needed caffeine to the system that would wake her up and hopefully make her feel better. Ahhh, caffeine, the number one drug in the world.

She could see that Brody hadn't bothered with breakfast at home, not even making coffee, although he had taken a shower and must have changed even though she hadn't heard him come into the room. He was another coffee bug, so he must have stopped for his java on the way into work.

Firing up the coffeemaker she went to make the bed while she waited. She combed her hair and put on a smudge or two of makeup before she sat down with a large mug of joe in the backyard. Della brought Miss Ezzy out for some sun, seeing as how it had finally broken through and it looked like a decent day ahead. That would fare well for the plans her parents had made. Della loved anything to do with Anne of Green Gables, so of course the visit would include a trip to everything Anne on the Island's north shore. The last time, Della had come home with the customary Island staple, a straw boater with red braids attached. They had gotten lots of pictures of her wearing it. She had actually worn it out, so she guessed there was a replacement in her immediate future.

Jill stretched her legs. How on earth was she going to be able to put on a cheerful face for her mother and father. She was not a good actress and her world was falling apart. Yet she had to pretend she never felt better in her life in spite of her anger. It bubbled just below the surface at the idea of another woman putting hands on *her* husband! And worse, Brody putting his hands on another woman. She felt nauseous at the thought of it and took a deep breath followed by a stiff hot drink of coffee. She would get through this somehow, try to understand, but there was a very good chance Brody would be carrying his head in his hand when he left this afternoon.

She'd been serious when she'd told him she hated him, because that's what she'd felt in the moment. Utterly and completely betrayed.

And there was little Della playing with her dolls without a care in the world. Jill had no idea how families navigated divorce when there were small children involved — or children at all for that matter. Would this end in divorce? Was that what Brody wanted? Is that what she wanted? And how did she deal with her anger, even at this point? True, the wound was still very fresh, having been inflicted mere hours ago. She'd never thought in a million years that Brody would stray. He was a great looking guy, everyone thought so, but he'd never tried to trade in on that. Typically unassuming he was not a man who felt the need to share himself with every pretty face that came along. No, he'd been totally devoted to her and she to him. This was an unexpected slap in the face.

True, she had yet to learn the extent of his betrayal and within hours she would. She was certainly not the first married person to face something like this, and wondered in that moment if her mother had ever gone through that with her father — or the other way around. She scanned memories of her growing up years but couldn't land on anything that hinted at such a dilemma. Her father was a handsome man, her mother highly attractive and they made a nice looking couple. Had her mother ever had to fight for her husband? Her parents had a strong marriage, but even the strongest of relationships had its challenges.

She took another gulp of coffee as unsettling thoughts continued to rumble through her tired brain. She had studied the wedding photo of her and Brody that she kept on the bedside table — fought the urge to smash the glass frame into a million pieces. Like her heart.

"Mommy, can I go over to the gazebo? Miss Ezzy said she wants to see it and she's never been there."

"Sure, go ahead, but stay where I can see you in the front. I'll watch from here."

"Daddy built that, didn't he."

"Yes, he did, dear."

"I love my daddy. He calls me Della Bella."

Jill forced a smile. "I know he does, honey, because he loves you very much. And your mommy loves you."

"Do you love, Miss Ezzy?"

"Of course I do. Now run along to the gazebo."

Della hesitated. "Why do you look so sad, Mommy? Why aren't you happy?"

"I'm happy, Della. Mommy didn't get a very good night's sleep last night. I'm a little tired is all. Take Miss Ezzy and go over to the gazebo."

Satisfied with her answer she scampered off, Miss Ezzy in tow. She could hear her talking to the doll, something about telling her to behave at Grandma's house. Good advice.

Jill downed the rest of her coffee, laying her head back in the overstuffed deck chair. Despite the caffeine she drifted off and was asleep only minutes when she came awake with a jerk. Della! Where was she!

Then thankfully she heard her little girl's prattle in the gazebo as she talked almost nonstop to her doll. With Della's penchant for running off lately she could have taken advantage of her mother's impromptu nap, but she hadn't.

Jill sat up in the chair and stretched. It'd been awhile since she'd felt as wretched as she did today. She heard the doorbell. Now who could that be?

Making sure that Della was still playing in the gazebo she hurried through to the front door. It had been the courier dropping off a package. Great! Della's toy had arrived in time to take it with her to her grandparents' house. Carrying the box inside she returned to the backyard and called to her daughter, announcing that her package had been delivered.

With a squeal of joy, Della and Miss Ezzy flew out of the gazebo and ran across the lawn into the house, following her mother through to the kitchen where the box sat waiting on the kitchen table.

"Can I open it, Mommy? Please?"

"Yes, but hold tight for a minute or two while I split the packing tape with a knife. Once I've got the tape off, you can look in the box yourself and pull out what's in there. Alright?"

"Okay, Mommy," she agreed dancing with excitement.

Once the box was ready she set it on the floor and Della reached in and pulled out the toy. What came out of that box shocked Jill to the core. What was happening!

Chapter 8

Instead of a plush purple octopus with pink hair, Della pulled out what could be best described as a vintage teddy bear, but not the cuddly fuzzy kind. This one was made of some type of knit fabric and its eyes, large and rounded, were as black as midnight. It appeared as though the original eyes had been torn off and the present ones reattached haphazardly over the holes left in the face. The nose matched the eyes and it too looked like it had replaced the original structure. Red paint had been smeared around the nose as though the bear had suffered some type of make-believe injury. On the battered lighter snout had been drawn a garish mouth in the same red paint, seemingly by a child's hand. It was a dreadful looking thing.

Della shrieked with delight, clutching the toy to her chest in an impossibly tight embrace. "I missed you so much. Look, Mommy, it's Bear Boy!"

Jill was momentarily speechless. "You know this toy?" she finally asked.

"Yes, Mommy. Don't you remember? I loved Bear Boy right from the start," and proceeded to scold the teddy bear for what had apparently been an overlong absence.

Jill's plan to return the bear because they'd shipped the wrong item was immediately set aside. Clearly this was the toy the child wanted, although it looked like something that had been discarded, or should be. And how had it taken the place of the purple octopus? This thing was large, coming nearly to Della's waist.

She'd thought the shipping box looked large for only a small toy. She threw up her hands mentally. Okay, goodbye one purple octopus, hello one very old teddy bear. Make that one creepy looking old teddy bear. Bear Boy, her daughter had called it. She watched as Della simultaneously hugged and kissed it, then held it at arms length to speak to it. The bear, of course, smiled that spooky smile that gave Jill the shivers. What possible explanation could the toy company have for this? What explanation could *anyone* possibly have?

Come to think about it, she *would* check this out, so while Della was still oohing and aahing over the bear, she opened her laptop and accessed her order history with the company. There it was, a picture of the octopus and the date it had been shipped. Someone had seen fit to play a prank at the warehouse, she assumed, but her daughter was delighted with it, so that meant it stayed. And the weirdest thing of all was that Della recognized it. This was beyond bazar!

Della carried the teddy bear into the living room and climbing into the recliner, sat the bear on her lap and began to rock back and forth. She glanced over at her mother with a broad smile. "Bear Boy is so happy to be home, Mommy. He said he missed me too. Wait 'til Grandma and Grandpa see him. They're going to be so happy. This is my favourite gift ever. Thank you, Mommy."

"I don't think it's going to be possible for you to take ahh ... Bear Boy with you to Grandma's house. You have quite a few toys packed as it is. What do you say you let him rest in your room while you're away. I'm sure he's tired from travelling all this way ... er ... back home."

"Noooo! I'm taking him with me."

"Della, your grandparents only have a small car. Now we've already packed what you're taking and you'll have Miss Ezzy with you. It wouldn't be fair to disappoint her now would it? So explain to Bear Boy that he'll have to do without you for a few more days. I'm sure he'll understand. But hurry and tell him because Grandma and Grandpa are going to be here any second. You might even want to go and tuck him in before you leave."

Della sighed, but at her mother's suggestion she explained the change in plans to Bear Boy before she reluctantly carried him down the hall to her room and, she assumed, put him in her bed.

Good! She'd hate to think what her parents would say for letting Della play with such a ratty old toy. Was it even clean?

Jill was relieved when her parents pulled up at last and Della threw herself at them for hugs and kisses when they stepped into the living room. She loved to go with Grandma and Grandpa, and the little girl would be kept so busy during her stay that she might not even give a second thought to the mysterious toy. That would be nice. In fact she'd put it away while Della was gone in hopes that she would forget about it altogether. Even better.

She was also glad to see them on their way before Brody arrived home, Della waving to her mother as they backed out of the driveway. Jill felt as tightly wound as a top at the moment. She'd seen her mother give her a worried look, although she was grateful she didn't verbalize her concern. Jill knew she would never be able to pretend that everything was all right between her and Brody if she'd been asked. Her mother would know immediately something was wrong, she may have even guessed as much already. She wouldn't make a good poker player. People could read her like a book. At least now the coast was clear so she and Brody could talk.

It was past 11:30 and Brody likely wouldn't be here for another few minutes, so hurrying down the hall carrying the empty shipping carton she pulled the bear off the bed and stuffed it unceremoniously inside. Once back in the kitchen she taped the box shut, angry at someone's idea of a practical joke. Wouldn't they have guessed the original order was for a small child? How many adults wanted a purple octopus with pink hair? None that she could imagine.

She made her way to the garage and standing on a stool, stuffed the box high on the top shelf in the corner. There, hopefully Della would forget all about *Bear Boy*. With any luck her mother and father would buy her a doll or a toy and she'd be off on a new adventure. She was counting on it.

Hurrying back to the house she made herself comfortable on the sofa. Her stomach was in knots and when the grandfather clock tocked out the noon hour, she took a deep breath to steady herself for the conversation that was to come. But still no Brody. He'd said he'd be here, but she had to take into account the travelling time between Summerside and O'Leary. Nevertheless, considering the unpleasant surprise she'd already received that had brought her to this point, she tried to prepare herself for anything. Would she be here all bright eyed and bushy tailed if it was her who was on the hot seat? Hardly, but then again she'd have enough sense not to get into this type of predicament in the first place. However, she warned herself yet again not to jump to conclusions, although in this case it was hard not to. She had to hear him out, for better or worse.

Her lack of sleep the previous night continued to catch up with her and she laid her head back. She didn't hear Brody come in, and it was him who gently shook her shoulder to wake her.

Blinking herself awake, she sat up straighter and picked up a cushion to hold on her lap, an unconscious desire to distance herself from her husband.

He settled himself into the recliner. At last they were facing each other for what Jill guessed would be one of the most unpleasant exchanges of her life. She drew first blood.

"When did your affair with this other woman start, Brody?"

He waited, the patient negotiator. "Let me start by saying I love you, Jill, and I never meant for this to happen."

The ice now broken, she jumped in with both feet. "So did she attack you and have her way with you when you weren't looking? Is that how it went?"

"Is there any need to be sarcastic?"

"When I'm angry ... in pain, I tend to be sarcastic, so the answer is yes. I'm definitely feeling the need. I asked you a specific question, Brody. How long has this been going on?"

He looked as though he wished he were anywhere else but sitting in that chair having this conversation. "A couple of months, I guess."

"How did it start?"

"How do any affairs start? At the beginning, I guess."

"Now look who's being sarcastic. I'm guessing you're the one who made the first move. And don't lie to me because I'll know. That little vein on the side of your head starts pulsing when you do and you can't control it. Was it you?"

He leaned his head back and closed his eyes. "No it wasn't me, but you might say I was ripe for the picking."

Outrage hurtled through her. "And what is that supposed to mean?"

"We agreed we were going to be honest with each other, Jill, and it takes two to tango. You work practically around the clock, meeting some deadline or other, and there hasn't been much going on in the bedroom as they say. You're always too busy or too something else. I guess I was feeling a little neglected ... ignored."

Jill swallowed her temper. "So this is all my fault. Why didn't you explain that earlier so we could avoid all of this unpleasantness. Poor baby got turned down a few times, what better excuse than to take a flight with the first bimbo that came along?"

And then another thought occurred to her. Maybe Amanda wasn't the first. "Is she your first or are you a serial cheater and I've been too busy, as you say, to notice. Or too stupid, because here I was thinking I had a sound marriage and the man I loved, no adored, would never think of playing around on me. I guess it sucks to be me, right?"

"Stop it, Jill!" he said angrily. "I am not a serial cheater. Did you ever consider that it's because I feel I don't deserve you because of the way I've hurt you."

She threw up her hands. "Why don't you admit that you screwed up, that you broke your marriage vows for a roll in the hay with another woman. Don't try to hide behind platitudes with me, Brody. In case you hadn't noticed, I'm not some dumb bimbo. I took vows before God when I became your wife that meant everything to me."

His colour rose. "You're not dead yet, Jill. You may find that somewhere along the road in that perfect life of yours you may make a mistake or two."

She laughed sardonically. "I guess we both know I already did when I trusted you."

"Okay, I'll give you that one," he said. "The poor boy from the wrong side of the tracks who made good, but who will never be good enough for the almighty Jill Sayer, the up and coming star of the theatre."

"You're jealous of me?"

"No, I'm not. This is coming out all wrong, but don't you see? I've never felt I was your equal. Your father told me as much when he first met me. He said you've got a long way to go to prove yourself, Brody, if you ever want to convince me you're good enough for my daughter. That's quite a ringing endorsement, don't you think?"

She stared at him. "You know, Brody, I never would have guessed you'd try to take the easy way out of a tight corner. The man I love has more going for him than that."

"Look," he said leaning forward, "we agreed to be honest with each other, so that's the not so pretty stuff that I wanted to get off my chest. Maybe I don't feel, way down deep, that I *am* good enough for you. But don't you ever dare say I'm taking the easy way out of this. I know I screwed up, in epic proportions, and I want to make it right."

"But isn't the gist of the whole thing that since I wasn't available for sex when you wanted it, you went out and found it somewhere else? That flies in the face of everything I thought to be true about you. *My* husband wouldn't do something like that!" She hugged the pillow and warned away the tears that threatened. "So tell me about this wonderful woman you're prepared to give me up for."

"Don't be so dramatic, Jill."

"Is it me or are you not grasping the gravity of this situation. This *is* dramatic, about as dramatic as it can possibly get. You've committed adultery, Brody. People get divorced over something like this."

He scrubbed his face with his hand. He did look exhausted. The snoring she'd heard could have been the only few minutes of sleep he'd managed to catch last night. Good. Let him suffer.

"So is that what you're saying? You want a divorce?"

She studied him before she spoke. "Boy wouldn't that make it easy for the two of you, because nowhere in here have I heard you say it's over with her, that you want me to forgive you. That it will never happen again. That your marriage is too important to you to lose."

He settled back in the chair. Were those tears in his eyes? "Would it do any good? You once told me that if such a thing were to ever happen you would divorce me in a heartbeat. I am trying to end the affair as a matter of fact, but I don't expect to be forgiven, Jill, not by you. I've heard you say a hundred times about how you're not the forgiving type, so why would I even ask?"

"Ahhh ... because it's important to you?"

"You're the expert with words. I can't compete with you in that regard. All I can say is that I love you with all my heart — always have, always will. No woman could ever touch that part of me that has been yours since the day we met."

She leaned her head back and expelled a pent up breath before meeting his gaze again. "Brody, you're confusing me. Let me ask you this, if we were sitting here talking about a marital indiscretion of mine, what would your reaction be?"

"I think we both know the answer to that."

"So how come you can't see how I feel? This affair you're having comes to light and the first thing you can think of is to say how it's really my fault because I wasn't giving you enough sex. Enough attention. But I will own that. You're right, I have an impossible career at times, chasing deadlines, and I can get preoccupied. Take on too much. I can see where you could feel you're coming in a distant second. That much I know to be true, and so for that I sincerely apologize. I admit that was a mistake and I truly regret it. I was aware it was happening, but I guess I thought everything would work itself out. I neglected you, and again, for that I am sorry. I was wrong. But Brody, there is never a scenario in which it's alright to step outside your marriage for another woman. I don't have to tell you that. That doesn't give you a gold card pass to cheat. If you're not going to hold yourself accountable, then I am. Are you in love with her?"

His response was encouragingly immediate. "No, I'm not in love with her. This is not a matter of the heart."

"Just sex then."

"I have never had sex with her, Jill."

She wanted to throw the cushion at him. Hard. "You're lying!"

He leaned forward. "I am not lying! I have never had sex of any kind with that woman."

She watched him. How could that be? "Okay, why not?"

"I just never went there, but she's pressuring me for it."

She hugged the pillow, her gaze unwavering. "So this is all about testing the water."

She knew she'd hit the nail on the head by the change in his expression. "I'm not shopping, if that's what you're implying, but yes, I admit I was playing with fire."

"Were you enjoying the chase ... or being chased? The attention? Seeing if you have it in you to actually make that leap to being a cheater?"

He folded his arms. "You're too damned smart for your own good but if it helps me any, I've learned that I can't be a cheater, not in the full sense of that word. I can't do that to you, and I can't do that to Della. I was loving her attention I guess. I knew it was wrong, of course I did, but you wouldn't understand what it means to a man to have the undivided attention of a beautiful woman. A woman that most men would give their right arm for. Unfortunately a woman who usually gets what she wants, and what she wants is to marry me."

She stared at him, her mouth open. This other woman was trying to take her husband away! "That's some path you've decided to go down. And I always took you for smart."

"Look, you got me, Jill! I totally admit to being swayed by a pretty face, flattered by her attention. I've been trying to keep it on a friends only basis but I can see now that it can't be done. I've let her know in no uncertain terms that I will never leave you, and there can't be anything between her and I other than friendship, but she's not paying attention."

"Answer me this, Brody. Have you seen her naked?"

Annoyed, he thrust his head to the side before looking at her again. "Why would you do this to yourself, Jill?"

"Answer my question please. Have you?"

"Yes, to try to seduce me. Amanda taking off her clothes is like anyone else taking off their shoes. She thinks nudity is freeing. So yes I've seen her naked. Once."

"And of course you looked the other way."

"Hell no, I looked and I will admit I was tempted. What man wouldn't be, but I didn't give in to it. It was then that I knew I was in over my head."

"You shouldn't have been there in the first place, to be tempted. I can see that she would naturally assume that since you were, you must be interested in having an affair."

"You're absolutely right, I shouldn't have been with her."

"Has she seen you naked?"

"Of course not. I haven't taken off a stitch of clothing in her presence. Fully clothed at all times."

"Well she missed a treat there."

"Very funny. In the interests of transparency I have kissed her, twice, and I

137

feel terrible about it. I knew this thing was starting to get out of hand and at first I didn't do much to try to stop it, but I am now. The trouble is, she's promised to keep trying to win me over and other than threatening her, I'm not sure what else I can do. I should never have encouraged her, but honestly, I thought she'd eventually lose interest and move on to someone else.

"That's what I meant when I said this wasn't what it looked like. I fully admit it looks very bad, and I was way over the line. My worst fear is that she'll try to involve herself in *your* life somehow, although I've warned her never to try such a thing. That's why I was late getting here. I spoke to her this morning and told her there would be no more lunches, or after-work drinks. No friendship, or anything that resembles it."

"So you haven't committed adultery, broken your wedding vows."

He sighed. "I'm sure there's something described in there that I'm guilty of breaching, but no, I have not slept with that woman — or any other woman, other than you. I came close, I have admitted that, but thank God I walked away. I know I was playing a dangerous game."

Jill didn't even try to stop the tears that spilled onto her cheeks. She felt the weight of him on the sofa beside her and tossing the lap cushion aside fell into his arms. And then he was picking her up and heading for the bedroom where they made love for the first time in weeks. If there was a sweeter experience this side of heaven, she was at a loss to imagine what it could be.

Later as they lay spent in each other's arms, they were still murmuring apologies for each of their shortcomings. They fell asleep like that, although it was a short respite and once again they reached for each other as the afternoon dwindled away.

"I've got to get back to the office," said Brody. "There is a supper meeting that I'm going to chair, so there's no way I can miss it. I'd invite you along if it was a couple's evening, but it's only us partners."

"Not to worry, I haven't done a thing on my play all day," she said, and explained about the new completion date. "But," she was quick to add, "we'll make time for each other. Let's never drift so far apart that it will be impossible to come back together. And please, Brody, don't ever do that to me again, even for a moment. Don't give another woman the opportunity to get her foot in the door. You're a hot guy, and because of that you're vulnerable. I can see that."

He chuckled. "I'm hot, am I? I'm glad you think so, Mrs. Sayer. I'd like to talk about how hot *you* are when I get back home tonight."

After another steamy kiss he climbed out of bed and headed for the shower. Within minutes he finished, grabbing a fresh shirt and much too soon was out the door leaving Jill to her thoughts. He'd promised to be home by nine or ten at the latest considering the meeting was taking place in Charlottetown, an hour and a half away.

She knew there were women who'd tell her she had been played for a fool. That she had let her cheating husband off the hook, but her gut told her he was telling the truth. That he had not slept with that woman was his saving grace. She wondered if she could find her way back if he'd actually been enjoying a sexual dalliance for the past two months. That could be a real deal breaker. But if there'd been no sex, why did he refer to it as an affair? It was likely just the wrong choice of words, so she dismissed it.

Stretching lazily, she knew she should get up and get back to work. She could begin to make a real dent in the Yeo mansion research in the next few hours, and that would be a tremendous help. But there was still so much to process about what had transpired during the past twenty-four hours.

She remembered when she'd first started dating Brody, the covetous looks of other women when they were out together. At the time it had made her feel proud that he was all hers. A friend had once told her not to worry about other women because surely she didn't want someone that no one else did. He was good-looking and sexy, so she'd become used to women casting glances.

It was also true that some women were aggressive enough to try to steal another woman's man. She'd met women who would do that at the drop of a hat, but she'd never been the victim of it before. The way Brody had described things, that's what was happening now. That Amanda had managed to turn her husband's head at all was a blade through the heart, but she had to move past it and allow their relationship to heal.

They'd made love hungrily this afternoon, reigniting the fire that had always burned so brightly between them. And now completely satiated, she felt sleep pulling at her so she gave in and closed her eyes. The room was in shadows when she woke again, and she felt weight against her back. She was not alone in bed. Brody had come home and slipped into bed with her, putting to rest any niggling doubts as to his sincerity. He loved her. He was back.

Still naked under the covers, she pressed her back against him. She and Brody loved to spoon, and she leaned into it now. But he didn't move. He must be asleep too. She turned, what better way to wake him than with a kiss? She wouldn't try to initiate sex, just cuddle with him since he wasn't naked, then they could get up and raid the fridge like they used to. Now that she thought about it, he'd already eaten at the supper meeting. Okay *she'd* raid the fridge.

Now facing him, her eyes still closed, she felt luxuriously sexy. She slowly opened her eyes, and a blood-curdling scream tore from her throat as she came face to face with Bear Boy.

Chapter 9

Jumping wildly out of bed she snatched up her clothes from the chair in the corner and sprinted out of the room, pulling the door shut behind her. Once in the bathroom she dressed quickly, then flipped on the outside light and started for the garage. She expected to see the empty shipping carton lying on the floor, but no. Climbing up on the stool as before, she saw it sitting on the top shelf precisely where she had placed it a few hours before. Without hesitating she pulled it down, angrily tore the tape free and there grinning up at her was Bear Boy, exactly as she'd stuffed him in. She stared at it for a moment before spying a roll of duct tape. Grabbing the roll she taped that box shut like she'd never taped anything shut before in her life. Brody had laughed when she told him about the toy mix-up, but it was no laughing matter. She never wanted to see that creature again.

It had apparently only been a bad dream, but never had anything appeared more real. Maybe instead of making an appointment for Della with her pediatrician, she should look for the appropriate professional and make one for herself. But were these lucid dreams where someone realized they were dreaming during their actual dream? She'd read about that, but all she knew was that she'd never experienced anything quite like what was happening lately. It was terrifying!

Taking a deep breath to calm her racing heart, she locked the garage door behind her and went back to the house. The first order of business was to open the bedroom door and remind herself that none of this was real. Sure enough, when she turned the light on there was the bed as empty as when she had leapt out of it. Even if she was one to believe in ghosts, that had still been some spectacular exit. Straight up in the air and out of there in under five seconds. She chuckled at the recollection of it. But once again she would not share any of it with Brody. Not after the face at the window thing, that poor man running around outside in the middle of a thunderstorm. He'd been remarkably good-natured about it, but it was nonetheless embarrassing. No, some things were best kept to oneself.

It was now nine o'clock and she was famished. Time to heat up a slice of that pizza.

The phone rang. Brody! Something important had been rekindled between them this afternoon and she was still on a high that even Bear Boy couldn't ruin. It was nice to think that Brody was too. She had been hungry for that reassurance and he'd delivered it in spades, but it wasn't Brody calling. It was her mother.

"Is everything okay, Mum?" she asked. "Is Della behaving for you?"

"She's a little angel of course, but I'm afraid your father and I are having a terrible time getting her settled down for the night. She keeps asking for something called Bear Boy. Do you know that toy?"

Jill groaned aloud. "Yes, I know Bear Boy. It's a horrible old beat up teddy bear that was sent to us by mistake from the toy site we usually use. I'm all for throwing it out, but Della took an instant shine to it. I guess there's no explaining taste, as they say."

"You know children, dear. They make up their own minds about what they like." She turned from the phone and spoke to someone, she assumed it was her father, before coming back on the line. "Your father is leaving now, Jill. He'll be there in a short while to pick up that toy. We've tried everything to settle her down, maybe that'll do the trick."

So back out to the garage she went and pulled the now hated package off the shelf, dropping it onto the floor. The box moved. Yelping, she jumped back.

"Jill!" she reprimanded herself. "The box tipped a little, that's all. Get a grip!"

Tearing the tape off the box, she hauled the teddy bear out and shutting off the light, marched back to the house. She was waiting for her father on the verandah when he arrived, and was only too happy to place Bear Boy in his hands.

"*That's* the toy that was shipped by mistake!" he declared.

"Yep! That's the toy she's so crazy about."

"Alrighty then," he shrugged as he looked at it disbelievingly. Giving her a quick peck on the cheek he was gone again within the minute.

Goodbye Bear Boy, and good riddance. She'd talk to her mother tomorrow to see if she could convince Della to let her new friend live with Grandma and Grandpa. It could wait for her there whenever she came to visit although she was sure her mother would be no more thrilled to have it in the house than she was. With any luck Della would go for the suggestion.

Now for that slice of pizza — a 10:00 p.m. supper. The nap had refreshed her, so she might as well wait up until Brody got home which should be any time now. As a partner in his firm there were several meetings a week to attend, and he'd more than once complained that for him, it was the downside of the corporate world. Sometimes he wondered, he'd said, if they spent too much time in meetings when that time could have been used more productively elsewhere. The monthly supper meeting was the one he disliked the most because when Brody ate a meal, he wanted to eat a meal, not talk half the way through it. He felt sorry for the person taking notes, trying to decipher what was being said as invariably people spoke with their mouth full.

Then another thought struck her. Hadn't their supper meeting been held two weeks ago? Or was it three? Either one, but it had definitely not been as long as a month ago. Doubt began to creep back in, but she did her best to ignore it. Was this the sort of thing that was going to start happening? Would she be able to get that old trust back? Of course she'd believed what he'd told her, but was that because she wanted to? Needed to?

"Jill!" She spoke sharply to herself, aloud, for the second time in an hour. "Stop this foolishness! You're overthinking everything, which you have a tendency to do. You're way too analytic, so stop it!"

On the heels of that reprimand, she squared her shoulders and polished off two slices of pizza.

Now 10:30, she decided to do a little more digging on Yeo House. In fact she'd go there tomorrow and spend some time. With Della away she should be able to make decent headway with the balance of her research and ideally get the framework up on the play itself. She'd pretty much decided that the name for the play would be Ghosts in the House? with the very meaningful question mark at the end. Of course she'd also give Jack some input on the name. He'd become a great friend during her short journey as a playwright. He'd even invited her and Brody to his wedding, he and his husband, Lucien, already happily together for many years.

Settling down on the sofa she opened her laptop and typed in Wheelie and immediately got a hit. It seemed there was even merchandise available now featuring the haunted dog. At least that's how he was referred to, making the most of his scary reputation. He was just as she'd remembered him, small but formidable. She also found another account of Wheelie's nocturnal escapades. As part of the original display that recreated how the child's bedroom may have looked in the mid to late 1800's, Wheelie would more than likely have been sitting on the floor since he was a pull toy. She remembered staff talking in the media about how they would find him moved to a different spot in the room from that occupied the previous day. That was actually Wheelie's major claim to fame. But by whose hand was he being moved during the night? So his location when they left for the day must have been documented in order to make the necessary comparison the following morning. But why only the bedroom? Perhaps she'd misunderstood, but if he was haunted, why not make a real night of it and travel throughout the entire house?

She smiled. He could have dropped down to see who was in the cooling casket.

Jill agreed that it would be unsettling for staff members to encounter such a thing as an eerily wandering toy, but her more practical side stubbornly emerged. Again, had someone held back that extra few seconds, to quickly move the wheeled toy, say onto the bed. She could picture the naughty grin on the face of the prankster when Wheelie's latest move was documented the next day. What fun that would be! The more famous Wheelie's adventures became, the more amusing it would be to maneuver the toy about. That would be a logical solution, but if people wanted to believe that somehow the toy was either moving by itself, or the hand of an unknown ghost child played with him when all was quiet during the night, so be it. It was a harmless enough pastime she supposed. And if Wheelie didn't mind the extra attention, earned or otherwise, what did it hurt? It had certainly been good for business as people came from near and far to see the famous little dog. Hadn't she?

She looked forward to her visit to the mansion tomorrow. She would pay particular attention to Wheelie, study him more closely because while she'd focus on Yeo House in her play, Wheelie himself would be the centerpiece. She too would take advantage of his popularity, which would in turn mean that her play might also get plenty of attention and that could never hurt.

Jill smiled as she let the play come to life in her mind with a life-size Wheelie. An actor in a Wheelie costume, complete with a damaged face, and on wheels of course. The gag value would be fantastic with intermittent appearances throughout the production. It could be very funny. And no matter what the toy dog said, it would be humorous. Actually, it might be funnier if he said nothing at all, just have him move around at will. The wheels under the life-size Wheelie would have to be motorized. She was sure Jack would have some ideas about that. She'd call him tomorrow and see when he was available for coffee. He would welcome any insights she could give him about the script so far.

The phone rang beside her and she jumped. Were her mother and father were still having trouble with Della? Her heart sank until she checked the caller ID and saw that it was Brody. He was on his cellphone. It was after eleven o'clock.

"Hey, baby," he said quietly. "I hope I didn't wake you."

"No, I decided to wait up. That's some supper meeting."

The hesitation on the other end of the line lasted too long. More than one heartbeat would have been too long. "Yeah, it's a long one," he said, "so it's probably best if you don't wait up. I know you have a busy day planned for tomorrow with that new deadline. You need your sleep."

"Don't you?"

"I'd like to crawl in bed right now, let me tell you. We finished up a couple of hours ago, officially, but there was some contentious stuff on the agenda so we're still at it. We're still talking, only now over drinks."

"And are you drinking, Brody, and planning to drive?"

"You know how I feel about that. I'm a sipper, so no worries there. I'm not going to take the chance and drive if I've had too much. But seriously, go on to bed, Jill. We'll catch up in the morning."

She sighed. "I had a good snooze after you left, so I'm wide awake. It's only eleven, and you shouldn't be too much longer. I'll wait up."

"Alright then, if you insist, but I'm not sure how long I'm going to be."

"I assume they close that place at some point."

"Sure two o'clock in the morning, but I don't imagine you want to wait up that late."

Jill didn't care for the sense of unease that had begun to flow through her. Still, she did hear the clang of glassware in the background. Brody was in a bar alright, but was it actually a meeting? She knew some meetings could go on indefinitely. It depended on what was up for discussion and how willing the group was to let go of whatever subject they'd gotten their teeth into. She guessed there wasn't much inclination to finish up anytime soon if drinks were now at hand. They were making an evening of it is what it sounded like, but who all was there? Did Amanda work at the firm? She must if he thought the receptionist had told Jill her name. Was she there tonight? With Brody?

She had to let it go. She would not lead her life suspicious of every move Brody made. He had explained himself to her satisfaction earlier, and now she would give him the benefit of the doubt, as she would expect the same from him.

"Jill, are you still there? Hello?"

"I'm still here," she said at length injecting warmth into her voice. "Like I said, I'll wait up, so I'll see you when you get home."

She could hear the smile in his voice. Had he felt the shift in her thinking? Probably. Couples in sync with each other often did.

"Great! Look, I'll get away as soon as I can, but there's a lot at stake with what's being said here. This thing started out as our regular monthly meeting, moved up a week because of vacations, but quickly blew up into something much more. Hopefully everything will settle down soon and then I'll be right along."

After she hung up from Brody she decided to do more digging about Yeo

House. She'd look into the Yeo family tree and was delighted to find numerous sites on the subject. Most featured James Yeo Sr. almost exclusively, before venturing into his descendants. Born in 1789, the son of a shoemaker, James Yeo Sr. began his working life as a labourer in either 1814 or 1815. Following the death of his first wife in 1818 he married again and the pair immigrated to Prince Edward Island in 1819.

She read on. He was described as an opportunist, but also a hard worker who, she decided from the available information, was clever enough not only to create opportunities to improve his lot in life, but to seize on others through backbreaking toil and unwavering determination. It was now apparent that it was the perfect combination to take advantage of an economically backward area at that time. By all accounts he was a formidable character with unflagging physical and mental stamina, the unyielding set of his mouth in a typically grim mid-life photo proof of his ruthless nature. He was considered to be the most prosperous man on the Island, and his hunger for wealth and prestige was also parlayed into politics. That became a successful career in and of itself and further cemented his sweeping power and influence.

Jill paused. This was interesting. It seemed that James Sr.'s second wife, Damaris, was equally as capable in business. In addition to bearing him seven children, five daughters and two sons, she "ably managed" her husband's stores, the largest on the western part of Prince Edward Island. Not surprising of those times, the Yeo stores were operated on a credit only basis, further indebting the people who worked for him.

All of this stuff was golden, perfect to help her develop the right feel for the play. She made a particular note that shipbuilding was just one of James Yeo Sr.'s several enterprises.

His son, James Yeo Jr., was also involved in shipbuilding and immensely wealthy as a matter of birth, and an appropriate status symbol would have been a mansion to house James Yeo Jr. and his family. And so in 1865 Yeo House was built, a three-story grand structure that boasted the requisite copula, in keeping with its Gothic Revival style. But curiously enough, while the rich typically had their fine homes constructed away from the sights and sounds of the labour yards that helped generate their wealth, James Yeo Jr. had decided to live within sight and sound of the family's shipyards. History does not explain why.

The Honourable James Yeo Sr. died in 1868, one year shy of his eightieth birthday. But James Yeo Jr. did make good on the political influence of his father, himself elected to the House of Assembly several times.

Hmmm... James Yeo Jr.'s brother, John, also enjoyed a sound career in politics, so the family was not unfamiliar with powerful influence. It seems James Yeo Sr.'s sons were able to build on the success of their father, the Yeo family holdings considered at the time to be the largest on Prince Edward Island.

James Yeo Jr. himself was hailed as a prominent businessman, most notably as a merchant, shipbuilder and ship owner. He lived to the ripe old age of eighty-nine, outliving his wife of fifty-eight years, Sarah, by four years.

James Yeo Jr. and Sarah (Glover) had six children, four sons and two daughters, and the only name known of those children she could find was Herbert, who died on the 13th of February 1903. Had Wheelie been *his* toy?

Jill closed her eyes and tried to envision a small child, likely a boy but possibly a girl, playing with the little toy dog on wheels. All that really remained of Wheelie's face were his eyes. Research material into a toy made during that era indicated a German toymaker who had used some type of thread to create the nose and mouth. It would seem that such material would be unlikely to withstand the rough play of a child. The pull cord too was long gone. What was left of the toy had been found in the wall. Discarded. Forgotten.

She loved doing research, and the more she read the more the play came to life in her mind. Now she'd see if she could find anything on James Yeo Sr.'s former residence. If the son James had been educated in Charlottetown, that might be a clue as to where the family had originally lived, although it seemed highly improbable. In those early days it would be a considerable distance to travel seeing as how the father's business interests were located far away on the western end of the Island. Even by today's modern standards it amounted to almost an hour and a half drive, in the latter part of the nineteenth century it would have been a much more demanding journey. History did record that James Yeo Sr. spent a great deal of time on horseback. But no, from what she was able to determine, James Yeo Sr. and his wife lived in Port Hill, Prince Edward Island, within a mile or so of where James Yeo Jr. built his lovely home. Were they a close family? They must have been, family gatherings likely a matter of routine at the Tyne Valley mansion. And now, more than a hundred and fifty years later, it was being celebrated for a much different reason than it's original intention of providing a suitably lavish residence.

Jill flexed her shoulders, deciding to call it quits for the night with her research. It was now a quarter after two, and she was getting tired. And hungry. Going to the kitchen she reheated the last slice of pizza and chewed each mouthful thoughtfully. Brody should have been home long before now. Even with a generous allowance for travelling time between Summerside and O'Leary, he was long overdue.

Halfway through the slice she lost her appetite and threw the remainder in the green garbage. The meeting excuse was beginning to wear thin, for her at least. She was tired of hearing about them. After all, most of those meetings that Brody had attended over the past two months had simply been a subterfuge for hanging out with Amanda. She understood that meetings were an important part of operating a business, but was it necessary to seek your partners' advice on every single move that was made in the run of a day? Okay, now she was descending into a really bad mood.

She decided to take a soothing hot shower because she was for sure going to wait up. Suppose he didn't get home for another few hours, she planned to be ready and waiting for him.

The shower was what she needed after being hunched over that laptop for hours, her cramped muscles relaxing under the powerful pulsing jets. She'd considered a tub bath, but she was prone to becoming a little too relaxed. The last time that happened she'd slid into the tub and awoke submerged with water up her nose. A shower would do just fine.

Once toweled off she pulled on a fresh cotton nightdress, brushed her teeth and made her way back to the living room to continue her vigil.

As she turned the corner there was Brody walking in the front door. She tried to read him. Tired was the first thing that came to mind.

Pulling off his shoes he headed for his recliner and flipped up the footrest, flexing his toes. "This is what I've been dying to do all night," he said stretching, "sit back and relax. You must be exhausted too. There was no need for you to wait up, Jill. I know my way to the bedroom."

What he had likely intended as humorous came out with an edge as she sat down and faced him.

One thing she was sure of, he was not intoxicated. He was not a drinker, a man who could spend hours in a bar, as it seemed he had tonight, and still stick to one or two drinks.

"What kept the meeting going until this late? I've never known one of your supper meetings to last so long."

"You'll never believe this, but the man who we've been trying to acquire as a client, has changed his mind it seems. The call came in to one of our partners while we were in the meeting. He'd actually flown to the Island in the hopes we could start up the process again. Naturally we were elated. He strikes a hard bargain but it's all but in the bag except for the signatures. It has been a very profitable evening for PE5 Financials. If there were any stores open on the way home I'd have stopped for a bottle of really good champagne and we could have drunk a toast. I'm so high I'll probably not sleep tonight. This is really big."

"That's fantastic, Brody! I know how hard you worked on this thing — the ups and downs, the big disappointment when the guy backed out the second time around. I just hope you're not riding for another fall. Let's hold off on the champagne until the documents are signed and your firm is actually managing his portfolio. When is that going to happen?"

"A few days. We have to get everything in order before we can do that. But I definitely feel it's going to happen this time, and that'll mean substantial bonuses for the acquisition team of which I am part."

"So the meeting wound up forty-five minutes ago? Wow!"

He coloured, and that was a dead giveaway. Brody was the worst liar in the world, and he knew it. "Not exactly."

Dread raced through her. "What do you mean, not exactly?"

"Is this the way it's going to be now, Jill? You running the clock on me, monitoring my every move?"

"I don't want to be like that, but do I have good reason to?"

He suddenly became way too interested in the weave of the chair fabric.

"You promised me transparency and now I'm taking you up on it, Brody. The meeting didn't go as late as you said, did it. I have a gut feeling you were with that woman." She refused to say her name.

He didn't look up. "Yes," he said at length, raising his eyes to meet hers, "I was."

Chapter 10

Jill felt the air whoosh out of her lungs. How could he have shared something so special with her this afternoon, convince her he loved her, and then do … this. She wanted to scream, she wanted to cry but mostly she wanted to throttle him. She understood at that moment how some domestic situations could escalate into violence, although she had no intention of acting on those impulses.

"I am so sorry for lying to you, Jill."

She managed somehow to keep her voice even. "It seems lying comes very easy to you these days."

"And I hate myself for it. The company meeting lasted until almost midnight, and yes, I think we've got that account in the bag. That's why this thing went as late as it did. What I haven't told you is that Amanda Leland, yes, *that* Amanda, is a partner in our firm. The golden girl come lately who was headhunted from a great school, and..."

"School! How old is she?"

"She's twenty-eight. She got her law degree then shifted gears and got a business degree. She started in university at the age of sixteen and was working on her MBA when

Don Sommers came calling. He talked her into joining our firm and completing her studies on the side. I wouldn't necessarily say she's man hungry but she's an over-achiever and I've found that also extends to her personal life. What I told you this afternoon was the absolute truth, but as I was afraid of, she doesn't want to let go."

"That implies there was something to let go *of.*"

"Nothing more than what I've already explained. Naturally she was there tonight and told me beforehand she wanted to speak with me after the meeting. So I thought great! She's finally listening. We can be cordial to one another from now on and let it go at that."

"Let me guess, she wanted you to come to her place."

"You're right, she did, but I told her no way, that this whole thing was a mistake and I accepted all the blame for allowing it to begin in the first place. But she wasn't having any of it. I don't think she'd do anything to cause me embarrassment and therefore also herself, but I doubt she's going to let it go. Meeting with her tonight was a mistake and I can guarantee it won't happen again. She says she has developed feelings for me and believes my future includes her. I have apologized to her for my part in this, as I told her I apologized to you. I told her I was done with the whole thing, said I was sorry for hurting her and left."

"And her parting words were...."

"You'll change your mind, or something like that. Jill, babe, once again, I couldn't be sorrier for bringing this into our marriage. I didn't plan to see her tonight. I wasn't even sure I would stay and speak with her, but after almost an entire evening of covert looks, parted lips and hair flipping I knew I had to do something. Make it clear to her that I have no intention of keeping this affair going. She's an intelligent young woman, certainly hard-nosed when it comes to business, so I thought she'd accept what I had to say and move on. Let's hope she does."

Jill could feel tension beginning to seep out of her. Brody had remained true to his word after all. "I wouldn't count on it. I've met her type before. Everything is all about her and I'm guessing there's a father in the picture who indulges her ... someone who has given her the idea that all she has to say is *I want...*"

"Grandfather."

"There you go. I'll stand beside you through this if you're telling me the truth, Brody, because sometimes things like this don't go away quietly. She likely won't."

He sighed tiredly. "I have told you the truth, but I'm afraid you're right. She's already proven she can be tenacious in the corporate world, but she doesn't know when to shut it off. I wish there was some way I could make up for laying this mess at your feet. You don't deserve it. If I was feeing ignored in the bedroom I should have found some way to deal with it other than what I did. Feeling justified in allowing another woman to get that close to me. I'm hugely embarrassed by this whole thing. I can't believe it happened because I've never been a want my cake and eat it too kind of guy. I guess we learn something new about ourselves every day. Now, I don't know about you but I've had enough of everything for one day. Let's go to bed."

She could see the exhaustion in his eyes. "Let's just hold each other, Brody, until we fall asleep."

"Sounds good to me," he said as they walked to the bedroom arm-in-arm.

Brody was snoring within five minutes of getting into bed, and the last thing Jill saw were the hands on the clock reading 3:15.

As usual Brody was up bright as a dollar at seven the next morning. It was the shower running that woke her, no make that his off-key rendition of New York, New York that brought her out of a sound sleep. The guy was tone deaf, but he loved to sing. Wasn't that the purpose of music anyway, other than the sheer joy of singing? It was only painful for those who weren't able to get out of earshot.

Slipping into her housecoat she tied it and went into the kitchen to start the coffee, then got bacon frying.

Brody joined her minutes later, freshly shaven, planting a kiss on her cheek before pouring himself a cup of coffee.

She kissed him back. "I'm assuming you have time for bacon and eggs because if you tell me you have to hurry off to another meeting I'm going to throw this pan at you," she told him, chuckling.

"Sure, I've got time for breakfast, and no, there's no early-morning meeting today. I would imagine some of the partners will be late getting in because their hats might not fit today — might be a little tight. I've never seen the point of doing that to yourself, drinking too much, and then complaining about feeling bad the next day. It's a self-inflicted wound, but to each their own."

Later, after a lingering, sexy kiss goodbye, Brody left for the day and Jill enjoyed the luxury of going back to bed for a couple more hours. It didn't take long to drift off, and she slept soundly until the alarm jangled her awake at eleven o'clock. She felt light, chipper, and not because of getting that extra two hours. Her spirit was at peace. She and Brody had weathered a storm and while she was still angry about him seeing that young woman, she forgave him. Now with any luck the whole thing would hopefully blow over, although she realized she was being naïve. Brody was a prize worth fighting for. She knew that from experience.

She thought again about him describing his friendship with that woman as an affair.

She'd meant to ask him why he had characterized it in that way, seeing as how the proper definition of an extra-marital affair was a sexual relationship. Even after he'd told her there'd been no sex between them, he continued to call it that. The devil was in the details, but she put it out of her mind annoyed with herself for digging up bones. It seems she too was reluctant to let something go. But still...

The phone was ringing when she got out of the shower. She hurried down the hall in a towel in case it was an emergency, but saw before it went to message that it was Della's pediatrician. Great! No need to pick up. She'd already explained the nature of her concern. It was simply a matter of being given an appointment. Sure enough, Della could be seen in three weeks time. Nothing much happened during the summer with vacations and all, and indeed Dr. Burgess had already left on holiday. This was not an emergency. The timeline would work perfectly.

She'd eaten a hearty breakfast, so passed on lunch and dressed lightly because it would be hot in that Yeo House today for her return visit. Off she set for the Green Park Shipbuilding Museum & Yeo House in Tyne Valley with her tape recorder, notepad, pen, and camera. Her father often teased her that she needed a large purse to carry all her money, but in fact it was a working purse, a utilitarian purse.

By the looks of it when she arrived at the complex, she was going to be alone in the mansion again today. That could be because of the excessive heat forecast for the Maritimes, and for sure it was a scorcher. She might change her plans to another day if she found the heat suffocating inside the house. It would be stifling on the upper floors.

Before entering she stopped to study the exterior as she had on her first visit here. What had it looked like upon completion of construction back in 1865? She wondered at any present day changes that may have been necessary to accommodate an alarm system to guard the valuable artifacts, while maintaining the building's historic integrity. She noted the angle of the sharply pitched roof, the eye-pleasing window frames rounded at the top instead of being unimaginatively straight. Wide shutters framed them perfectly. She loved the gabling. She thought of it as gingerbread but she could be wrong about that. Not being an architect, these things escaped her, but she did appreciate the octagonal cupola that sat on the roof like a beautiful cake top ornament. The verandahs were generously wide and inviting. She could imagine the family in bygone days congregating there on fine summer evenings not far from the sparkling waters of the Strait.

Moving on into the interior of the home she'd been correct in assuming it would be stuffy, but found it tolerable. Stopping to view each room from behind the stanchioned rope barriers, she snapped pictures, made notes, gathered impressions, and listened closely to the interpreter's narrative. However today was also about getting a feel for the place, allowing herself to be transported back in time to a hundred and fifty years ago. Trying to envision the day-to-day lifestyle of those who had once called the Yeo mansion home.

She thought about household servants seeing to the needs of the family, as was the practice for those who were wealthy enough to afford them. What had their lives been like? It was easy to imagine the drudgery of the servants' work, but what of those whom they served? There was limited resource material about that particular experience. Access to any Yeo diaries from that era that might have existed would provide an absolute goldmine of information. What a stroke of good fortune it would have been to find something like that hidden in the walls, but no mention had ever been made of such a thing. The lady who guided her today did tell her about an upcoming ghost tour. Now that was something she'd be interested in, so she'd sign up before she left. She would feel like a bit of a hypocrite, but she wouldn't let on she was a disbeliever and ruin anyone else's good time. Ghosts were where you found them, in your imagination, and she couldn't think of anything that would change her mind about that.

They were now at the parlour and the guide explained it had been set up for a wake, which included that enchanting piece of décor, the cooling casket. Jill supposed it was a grim reminder of what eventually awaited us all, but she wouldn't want to have to look at it every day or even know it was stored somewhere on the property. It'd be like living in a morgue. How long had deceased loved ones been left to cool in it? Her research had revealed it was also used to transport the body from home to the funeral parlour, and thus delay decay. It also kept animals and flies off the dead body. Ugh!

Once she'd given the first floor a proper going over, it was time to move upstairs, and she assured the very congenial staff member that she was fine at this point to look around on her own. Jill was aware of what she would see, her original visit cut short by Della's flip out over Wheelie.

Jill advised the interpreter that she wanted to quietly observe from this point on, because she was working on a project that included her impressions of the building and its contents. The interpreter wished her success with her project, and graciously withdrew.

The carpeted stairs creaked as she climbed slowly to the second floor and first made her way to the other bedrooms before backtracking to the aforementioned child's bedroom. This was Wheelie's turf, and there he stood in his plexiglass box with that same frightening face. How Della could have been drawn to such a ghoulish toy was beyond her. But then look how she'd taken to Bear Boy, like he was some long lost friend. And hadn't she called Wheelie by another name? Oh yes, Punch Willigan. She must ask the guide on her way out if that name meant anything in terms of the history of the house. But, she reasoned, if they'd had an actual name for him they likely would have called him by that instead of Wheelie, so she wouldn't bother inquiring.

She thought about James Yeo Jr.'s son, Herbert, who had lived in this house. How old had he been when he passed away. Had he grown to adulthood, or had he been a late in life child? If Wheelie had belonged to him, had they hidden his toy dog away in a wall because they could no longer bear to look at their son's favourite plaything? Anything was possible.

The two wooden toys on the floor could have been made by the same toymaker in Germany who had created Wheelie. Had the toys been imported via one of the Yeo family's ocean-going ships? There was no online toy company in those days, or any online at all, so toys had to find their way to market from Europe by sail. Or travel could have been a penchant for a Yeo family member, each toy lovingly chosen for their children in a quaint toyshop in Germany.

She could imagine what Christmas morning would have been like. For certain not the avalanche of playthings as was most often the case for children these days. In all likelihood one or two nice pieces for each person had found their way under an elaborately festooned Christmas tree.

Her cellphone vibrated and she checked to see who it was. Jack Rinsky, the director. She'd take the call.

"Hey, Jack. What's up?"

"Got your message, darling. Yes, I'm free for coffee tomorrow and I agree it'd be helpful to discuss where you're going with this thing so far."

Jack Rinsky was an accomplished playwright in his own right until he'd fallen in love with directing. She had already learned a great deal from him and welcomed the opportunity for more guidance.

"Perfect! I'm at Yeo House today, letting the place seep into my bones. Della's off with her grandparents for a few days, so I'm grabbing that opportunity to really take a good look around. Actually, I'm signing up for a ghost tour before I leave today. I'm in the zone."

"That's my girl. Can hardly wait to pick your brain about this."

They agreed on where to meet and Jill returned to her observation of Wheelie after the call was ended. Looking at the plexiglass box, she focused her attention on the toy dog on wheels. It was the strangest thing. He seemed to be staring right at her. Kudos to a skilled toymaker, even way back then, to be able to create such lifelike animal eyes. Solid black, yes, but there was a depth to them that she hadn't really noticed before. The front of its face being damaged the way it was, the nose and mouth missing, gave it an otherworldly appearance. Creepy was the word that insisted on coming to mind. Not haunted, just creepy.

She turned her attention back to the carved rocking horse, and admired the detail, including its dapple-grey coat and real horsehair tail. But there wasn't the same connection, an unsettling feeling that washed over her when she studied that toy as there was when she looked at Wheelie. Despite the dog's small stature, a fraction of the size of the rocking horse, he easily dominated the room. She felt that might have been the case even before he became famous for being freed from a wall, as well as the hijinks he'd gotten up to since gaining his freedom.

She switched her gaze back to Wheelie. She stopped short. That thing had changed its position in the box, she was sure of it. He'd been facing toward the toy horse and now he was looking in the opposite direction. No, that couldn't be! Remaining behind the barrier, she knelt down to the same level of the plexiglass box a short distance away and adjusted her line of vision until she was looking him straight in the eye. Her breath caught. There was expression in those eyes. That dog appeared to be studying her with his bottomless black eyes. It was more than a little disquieting.

Raising to a standing position she decided to switch her attention to the doll. See if she felt an attachment to it too. But no matter how she tried to free her mind, think about the age of the doll and the Victorian-era children who had played with her, she was still a paper mâché doll with a blank expression sitting in a tiny wooden doll chair.

She felt satisfied with what she had accomplished everything she had set out to here today. She turned to go but could not resist one last look at Wheelie. She stared incredulously. That toy dog had shifted his position in his plexiglass enclosure yet again. He was now directly facing the door. But how was that possible? She clearly needed to get more sleep. She was still seeing things.

Descending the stairs, still absorbing the atmosphere, she hoped to find one of the guides to ask about the toy dog. And then she heard it, an other-worldly shriek! Upstairs from where she'd just come. It sounded as though it was in one of the bedrooms. She felt the hair rise on her arms and the back of her neck. It was probably the wind blowing in the cupola, but she felt a strange presence. It was something that if she tried to describe it, she wouldn't be able to. It was a feeling, a ... presence. She shook it off. The heat in this part of the building was suffocating. Anyone would feel a *presence* on such a hot day.

On the way out she spied the same staff member who had interpreted for her earlier and told her about what she'd heard. The reply was that such a thing had been heard many times before, and agreed that it was unsettling.

Jill had to admit that it was, although she still didn't completely dismiss the possibility that someone was playing a trick. Or it could have been as she'd originally thought, simply the wind. In any event, this was all part of the ride. She also wondered whether Wheelie had been observed changing positions within his plexiglass box. If he couldn't move about the room as freely as he'd once done, was he making do within his present confines? She prided herself on having about an open a mind as it was possible to possess, and she knew what she had seen — or more to the point thought she had seen. It was true the eyes played tricks at times and that was especially true if a person was tired or under stress. She could easily check both those boxes over the past few days.

So she signed up for the haunted tour before she left, paid her money, and knew the experience would help round out what she'd already been able to unearth about Yeo House. She was hoping it would provide a wealth of new material, not to mention that it'd be a lot of fun. It was a godsend that Della was with her grandparents. That gave her the opportunity to get all of this stuff done. Della wouldn't have been old enough to accompany her mother on the ghost tour, but even if she was of age, Jill had no plans to bring her daughter to this house again for any reason. She had yet to fathom why the little girl had acted the way she did with Wheelie. She couldn't get that out of her mind.

Glancing back at Yeo House while she waited for the AC to cool down the interior of her car, she realized how relieved she was to leave the nineteenth century behind. She'd treat herself to an ice cream on the way home, the Island famous for its favourite brand. She chose triple cherry fudge, a double since she'd never had to watch her weight. Finding a bench in the shade outside the ice cream shop she got to work on the delicious treat. But she had to work fast, the heat melting the ice cream almost as fast as she could lick. So she moved into the air conditioning of her car to enjoy the rest of her cone at her leisure.

Someone tapped on her window and she looked up into the face of her friend, Paula. Jill motioned for her to come sit in the car.

"It's nice and cool in here," said Paula climbing in and reclining her head against the headrest. "And that looks good what you're eating. What's the flavour?"

Jill told her and Paula moaned. "You know, if I wasn't on a diet, again, that's exactly the flavour I'd get."

"You look like you've lost weight."

Paula beamed. "I did, twenty and a half pounds already, so I'm not going to jeopardize my self-control by giving in to an ice cream today. I know me, if I cheat once I'm lost."

"Yeah, I'm lucky. I can usually eat what I want."

"You're tall so you can get away with it. There's more room for the weight to go, and on you, Jill, it goes to all the right places. On me it goes straight to my butt, no detours. Anyway, I was passing by and saw your car, thought I'd stop and say hi. I ran out for some tomatoes to make a salad. I forgot to put them on my grocery list so I'm on my way to the market. Gotta go! Mitch is waiting," and the two women made plans to get together soon for coffee.

She wondered how Paula and Mitch were making out. Her friend seemed happy, so she figured their marriage must be back on an even keel. She didn't want to mention anything about her own bump on the marital highway. She'd rather not share that with anyone. Even if they'd broken up over it, she wasn't into revealing personal details. In any event it didn't matter because they'd managed to get past this, or were in the process of doing so. Brody had made a mistake. It wouldn't serve any purpose to keep throwing it up in his face. It was impossible for something to heal if it was constantly being torn open.

Her ice cream now down to the pointy part at the bottom of the cone, she popped what was left in her mouth and enjoyed it to the very last bite. She could eat her weight in ice cream.

The drive home was uneventful, until she turned in to her driveway. There was a strange car sitting there. Who could that be? She spied someone sitting in one of the wicker chairs on the verandah as she grabbed her purse and hurried to the front door. A woman got to her feet when she saw Jill approaching and extended her hand, smiling.

"Hi, you must be Jill. I recognize you from your picture," she said as she shook Jill's hand. "It's great to finally meet you. I'm Amanda."

Chapter 11

Jill's mouth fell open, she could feel it, but she quickly recovered, snatching her hand back. "You've got a nerve coming here. What do you want?"

"Can we go inside and discuss this rationally?"

"No, we may not go inside because there's nothing to discuss, rationally or otherwise. I want you to leave."

Amanda sighed as she let her hand drop to her side but remained poised. However Brody might have described her he would not have done her justice. She was strikingly beautiful. Her skin was bronzed and flawless, her hair like black silk, her eyes wide, expertly accentuated, and the most unusual shade of amber she'd ever seen. She was tall with womanly curves and appeared to be urbanely sophisticated – even her clothes were effortlessly chic. In order words, Jill thought, she was everything she, Brody's wife, was not. Rationally speaking, as Amanda might say, she understood why this woman had turned her husband's head. Any man would be flattered by Amanda's attention, but that didn't make Jill any more amenable to the situation.

But the young woman did not in any way come across as condescending. She actually seemed friendly.

"Can't we at least sit down?" she asked Jill quietly.

Jill shook her head. "No, I want you to leave. I mean it. There's nothing you and I have to talk about. I am Brody's wife. You are not. Goodbye."

Amanda took a deep breath. "He's playing both of us you know. He's promised to marry me, and I'm guessing he's been telling you there's nothing between him and I besides friendship, which is categorically untrue. We've been lovers for a while and I'm deeply in love with him, and he tells me, often, that he loves me. He's probably telling you he loves you too. Am I right?"

The triple cherry fudge ice cream instantly soured and she worked to keep her stomach down. She felt as though she'd been pushed into the deep end and forgotten how to swim.

"I don't believe a word you're saying," Jill said, surprised at how steady her voice sounded. "I know my husband, and he's not the liar you're making him out to be. If anyone's lying here, it's you. He's already warned me that you might make trouble after his conversation with you last night. He said you wouldn't give up easily and I can see he was right, but this is one time that no means no."

Amanda chuckled. "And to me he's saying he wants desperately to tell you it's over but can't bring himself to do so, right now, but that he will ... soon. He says he's afraid you might make trouble for *me*, damage my professional reputation in some way. That's why I came here to have this conversation, woman to woman. Really, we have to stand up for one another. We have to have each other's backs, even when it's a difficult situation like this. Your husband is a player, Jill."

"My name is Mrs. Sayer," Jill countered.

Amanda smiled at her wistfully. "I can understand why that name means something to you. Brody did say you were still desperately in love with him and I'm sorry for that. It's sad, but I think it's also important to know when to let go. He calls me the future Mrs. Sayer. He said that last night after we'd made ... well you get the picture. He told me to be patient because he's concerned about his child, and how she'll take the breakup. He plans to seek full custody whenever he does ask you for a divorce, and I couldn't be more delighted. I love children. I will make an excellent mother to Della. I keep telling him it will be a smooth transition, so not to worry. But he cares for his little girl very much and he feels sorry for you."

Jill held her ground. "You are a very practiced liar, but I don't believe a word that's coming out of your mouth."

"Hmmmm. Brody told me you were stubborn, so I brought proof. They say one picture is worth a thousand words."

"Right, some photoshopped naked picture of him? Do you think I was born yesterday?"

Pulling her phone from her purse Amanda scrolled to an image then turned the device so Jill could look at it. She had to move it further into the shade to see it more clearly, and there smiling back at her was Brody and Amanda together. There was no mistaking Amanda's stunning face and that was certainly Brody. She recognized the shirt he was wearing. She'd given it to him for his birthday. Amanda's hand lay against his chest possessively and his arm was around her, his hand cupping her shoulder to draw her close. It looked as though they were about to kiss. This was obviously a selfie, so Brody would have been aware the picture was being taken.

"So?" Jill asked bravely.

"So! This is proof that we're together. The way he feels about me is quite apparent in this image, no matter how much he's managed to convince you that nothing's going on between him and me. Or more to the point that perhaps there once was but isn't anymore. It's all a tissue of lies. And let me guess, he's probably told you that he and

I have never been intimate. If he has, that would be another lie. As I've already told you, we made love just last night. He didn't stay as long as I'd have liked him to. He said he'd promised you he'd be home at a certain time. It was getting late and he didn't want to upset the applecart yet. Those were his very words.

Believe me, I know every inch of your husband's body intimately. We are not casual lovers. The chemistry between us is off the charts, whereas with you, to put it in Brody's words, the fire went out a long time ago. He only has sex with you out of duty. He *makes love* to me with genuine desire. Now, I can tell you're an intelligent woman, so why would you want to hold onto a man who no longer wants you?"

Jill had no other inclination at the moment than to fight back, to wound this woman as badly as she was hurting her. It was a primal response. "And why do you want a man whom you call a player? How do you know he's not playing around on you. I'm sure you've heard the old adage if they'll do it with you, they'll do it to you. You're nothing but a willing woman. A woman with a price. No substance whatsoever."

Amanda's hand flew up to connect with Jill's face, but Jill, ever the athlete, grabbed her before she made contact. "You know what your problem is, Amanda? You haven't got sense enough not to stand too close to the fire."

Amanda snatched her hand out of Jill's grip and took a reflexive step backward. "You're a real amazon aren't you? I can see I underestimated your strength, but there will be a price to pay for that last remark. I can see very clearly now what Brody has to contend with because in addition to a deep freeze in the bedroom, you're common. It's written all over you. Can you honestly blame him for choosing me over you? There's no comparison. I have class. You have none. Look at you, cotton shorts and a tank top. Flip flops. Hair hauled back in a ponytail, no make-up. You're a mess, about as unsexy as a woman can get. What about you would ever attract a man like Brody I'll never understand. Did you tell him you were knocked up? Is that how it went? And here's an old adage for you, madam. You cannot make a silk purse out of a sow's ear. It simply cannot be done."

Jill did not feel any better despite the exchange of venom. No release. "I told you to leave. Get off this property or I will call the police and have you removed for trespassing."

Amanda shook her head slowly. "You know I actually feel sorry for you, not because of what you're not and never can be, but because you've already lost Brody and don't even know it yet. You're still clinging to the hope that you can turn this thing around, am I right? How many times are you going to buy that *I have to work late* story?" Unbelievable!"

"I said leave!"

"Denial can be very debilitating. You can't live your best life if you're still wallowing in lies you're determined to tell yourself. You know, and this is just my personal observation, if you can't even be honest with yourself, what else have you got? And now you're going to have to tell a bunch of lies to that little girl of yours to try to poison her against me, but at the end of the day, will you really like yourself? See I think you've been in denial for a really long time.

"I think we can both agree that Brody is a gorgeous man, tall, dark, handsome and oh so sexy. Have you ever looked in the mirror and realized you're no match for such a good-looking man, you being so plain? And before you bother to defend yourself, I've seen the wedding picture. He has it on his desk with the other family photos. My first impression when I saw it was that you were passably pretty, at best, but now that I see you in person, I have to give full credit to whomever did your makeup for the big day. He, or she, managed to work wonders. It makes for great pictures, but in real life that makeup has to come off at some point. If this is what Brody has to look at every day..."

Jill's gaze never wavered. "You're a spoiled brat and my guess is that you've led a very sheltered life, with a sugar daddy in the closet somewhere – whether or not he's related to you I have no idea. That's your skeleton to live with, but if you think that you can choose some other woman's husband to take for your own, you're way off base."

Amanda slipped her phone back into her Gucci bag. At least there were no more photos to share, but what did it matter at this point. What she did show her was incriminating enough. She'd trusted Brody, believed him, but some of the things this woman was saying certainly cast serious doubt on *his* account of things.

Amanda folded her arms. "I came here today in good faith as I've already explained. I thought I could possibly spare you the pain of holding onto a man who's lost interest in you. That you are routinely being lied to, but instead of gratitude you verbally attack me."

"You're delusional."

"And I can say the same about you. Take the blinders off, *Mrs. Sayer*, he doesn't want you anymore. He's told me more than once that he's never felt so satisfied in bed. I will admit it took me a while to get him there because he likes to play hard to get, but now he can't keep his hands off me. It's embarrassing."

"From what I hear you can't keep your clothes on, for any man I assume, not just my husband. You like nothing better than the sound of your clothes hitting the floor."

Amanda threw back her head and laughed. "Once again, wrong. Your *husband* loves the sound of my clothes hitting the floor, like he did last night. I usually don't get a chance to undress myself. He does it for me. He gets so excited I'm afraid he's very hard on buttons. And I don't even get to return the favour because he tears his own clothes off pretty fast too. I'm telling you we're like maniacs when we want to get at each other, very often we don't even make it to my king sized bed. If we don't, and lust has its way, we make up for it when we do get there with lovemaking that I could only dream about before I met Brody."

Jill was immediately reminded of the buttons she'd found missing off Brody's shirt. She'd assumed it was poor workmanship at the factory. That could happen. She wouldn't condemn a man for some missing buttons. She'd never seen any evidence of his clothing been torn or damaged in any way.

Amanda's smile had gone cold. She'd be a deadly combatant in any type of confrontation. "Getting back to your wedding picture, I'd say Mommy and Daddy had to cough up quite a bundle for that overdone gown. It looked like the perfect fairy tale wedding, but in reality, the only thing fairy-tale about it is your make believe marriage. It's not what you think it is at all.

"And by the way, do you know I'm not the first? From what I hear around the office your bad boy husband had an affair with one of the administrative assistants who worked for him when he first went there. I think her name was… My gosh! Come to think of it, her name was Amanda too and she fell head over heels for him. She not only left the company, but also left town. Rumour has it she was pregnant, but you know how people talk. She was probably upset that she had to take the brunt of the entire mess. Brody skated out of another one, but he could have lost his job over it.”

“Again, if that’s the way he is, why do you want him?”

“People make mistakes and I’m not really one to beat someone up over a less than delicate past. I am a very intelligent woman and I have sense enough to know when someone is lying to me — which I think you might too although you refuse to see the truth. That’s equally as bad, but I digress. Brody has convinced me that he’s deeply in love with me. I believe him, and I’m the one who can tame him. I also believe he’s a gentle man, despite his decisive personality. He doesn’t like hurting people, and that would be you. He dreads the blow-up. He did speak to me last night about letting things lie until the time is right, but I have a habit of taking the bull by the horns. I know he’ll appreciate my coming here because it will speed up the inevitable. He wants what I want, for us to be together and to have the whole nasty divorce thing over and done with. If I’ve helped expedite that in any way, then all he needs to say to me is thank you. All I need to say to you, is good luck. You’re going to need it.”

Amanda turned on her heel and walked elegantly back to her sports car. She didn't even seem bothered by the heat.

Jill knew that if she were a volcano instead of a woman, she would have already had an eruption of epic proportions. As it was she had held herself in tight control. She was not a violent person, nor would she lower herself to assault anyone. It was wrong for a long list of good reasons. She would not give up her sterling reputation for something like this.

She was perspiring heavily when her shaking legs took her inside, an anomaly seeing as how cold chills were racing up and down her spine. She sank onto a kitchen chair, numbness settling into her bones. She could barely think through the grey fog in her brain. So who was lying to her? Her first instinct was to believe her husband, but Amanda had also stood before her and recounted events that held the ring of truth. She seemed to know Brody well. There had been another Amanda at the firm who'd quit and moved away, although she couldn't recall the backstory at the moment.

And then there was that picture. That had been all too real. Amanda and Brody, together. Did he think she would never see it? Friends indeed! The truth had a way of coming out, and so it had. She remembered Brody's word, *affair*. She barely made it to the bathroom before she was sick, and as she sat, her face pressed against cool porcelain, the sobs came in huge gulps.

Finally spent she washed her face with a cold facecloth and brushed her teeth. She felt like going for a run, a soul-pounding ten kilometres that would help her find centre again. But it was simply too hot out today, so why add heat stroke to her misery because no matter what might lie ahead, she had to stay healthy for her little girl. She was a mother first and foremost. Husbands ... boyfriends could come and go, your child was your child forever.

But she needed a run, desperately, to release some of that awful anxiety that was boiling inside her. So turning up the AC in the exercise room she laced on her runners, cranked up the speed on the treadmill and set off for parts unknown. Her favourite rock group blared from the speakers as she ran and ran and ran. At last, physically exhausted but mentally refreshed, she slowed the machine and walked the last kilometre. Then she hit the shower — cold and revitalizing.

Toweling off she dressed in clothes that Amanda had described as *about as unsexy as a woman can get*. No class. Whatever. Give her cotton any day. She didn't have time or the inclination to run around in silk with perfect makeup and manicured nails. She looked at her nails. They were fine. She would admit that her hair was untamed at best, naturally curly and tumbling over her shoulders. Brody had often told her he loved it that way. So did she, so that's the way it would stay. She was not a girly girl constantly beautifying herself. Not that there was anything wrong with that, but it wasn't her. She was a soap and water kind of girl, like her mother before her.

Having also inherited her mother's steely resolve she finished dressing and forced herself to eat something. She chose dry toast and an orange. She couldn't even consider anything else.

Next she called her mother, hoping for her calm soothing voice on the other end of the line. She wasn't ready to share any of this with her, not yet. She wasn't even at the wound licking stage, still completely gutted.

"Hi Mum," she said when her mother answered the phone. "How's everything going there?"

"I will say we've had our moments, but I don't let her off with anything. Like any child she can be demanding."

"What happened?"

"She is a sweet natured child, but when she gets hold of that teddy bear it's a different story. She can be quite naughty, but you know she apologizes later, so all is forgiven."

Jill took a deep breath. "I'm glad you're calling her on her bad behavior. She likes to push the envelope sometimes, but I don't know what to do about that bear. He's hideous, but Della instantly bonded with it so I can't yank it away from her and burn it."

Her mother laughed. "I share your sentiments. I thought maybe it wasn't even clean, but I did manage to pry it away from her. I gave it a good going over and it doesn't have any odor. It doesn't feel soiled either, but heaven only knows where it came from."

"At least it's keeping her occupied."

"That's another thing. We had activities planned for our time together. We wanted to take her shopping for a new Anne of Green Gables doll, we'd even planned a day at the beach but she's not interested. Told us flat out she doesn't want to leave Bear Boy behind. I'm serious. So naturally we told her he could come along but she told us he didn't want to go so she couldn't either. It's unbelievable, so here we sit in our backyard. She doesn't even want to go out to lunch, just stay here with Bear Boy."

Jill shook her head. "Bear Boy alright. I seriously would do something with it if Della weren't so attached. Has she played at all with Miss Ezzy? She was everything to her before that awful teddy bear showed up."

"That's another crazy thing. She brought her Miss Ezzy doll to us and asked us to throw it away. She doesn't want her anymore. She said Bear Boy told her to do it and she has to do everything he tells her."

"She said that about Miss Ezzy! I can hardly believe what I'm hearing."

"Believe it. And who is Punch Willigan by the way? Anyone I know?"

Jill sighed audibly. 'That's a whole other story. I think we have another writer in the family because that child has such an active imagination." She told her mother about Della's reaction to seeing the Wheelie toy at the Yeo mansion.

"Wheelie! I read about him. Your father and I have been meaning to get down to Tyne Valley and look around. I thought that little toy was so cute, in an off-putting sort of way. I guess Della thought the same thing. They say the toy is haunted."

"Right. A haunted toy."

"There are documented cases of that happening you know, although I give such a thing a lot of latitude. I don't think you believe in ghosts at all, do you dear?"

"Nope! Not at all. Everything has a logical explanation, although sometimes it takes a while to discover what it is. My next play is a spoof about that very thing. I'm researching all of the *haunted* places on the Island and having a good laugh at all that hype."

"Won't you be popular with Island tourism."

Jill laughed and it succeeded in dispelling some of her tension. "They'll probably run me right off the Island when it's staged in the new year. Or who knows, they might even come to see it, because it'll likely bring their so-called haunted places a lot more media attention. That is if the play is a success. Nothing like a good comedy to loosen people up and help them see things another way. That's all I am, another voice, another viewpoint."

Her mother laughed too. "And I'm willing to bet there are one or two things niggling at you that you've discovered in your research that you haven't been able to explain away. Are you having a good time writing this?"

Her mother knew her too well. "It's interesting for sure. This play is for skeptics and I hope they enjoy it. It'll be great if whoever reviews it for the media is a skeptic too. Anyhow, Mum, put Della on the phone for a few minutes. I need my Della fix for the day."

"I'm afraid she's sleeping, dear. We had trouble getting her settled down last night and she was falling asleep at the table at lunchtime. Let me go in and see if she's awake. She could be in there playing. Hold the line."

Della did come and after a short conversation, because Bear Boy was waiting, Jill rang off with a promise to call her the next morning. She had no sooner hung up when it rang again. It was Brody.

"Hiya, babe," he said cheerfully. "Just wanted to let you know I'll be a little late tonight. It looks like that big client is finally in the bag. I'll stop for a bottle of champagne on the way home, but it could be a while."

Jill's voice sounded flat, even to her. "Don't bother with the bottle of champagne, Brody. Matter of fact, don't even bother coming home."

Chapter 12

Silence on the other end of the line. "I beg your pardon?"

"I think you heard me clearly enough. I'm saying find somewhere else to sleep tonight, I don't think that should be too hard for you to do. I've got to go, Brody."

"What's going on, Jill! Why are you telling me not to come home? Did something happen that I'm not aware of because right now you're not making any sense at all."

"Really? Look, Brody, go to your … meeting. Stay as late as you want, but I'm telling you I don't want you to come home."

"You can't tell me not to do that! It's my home too, dammit, and if I want to come there after I finish work I will," he said angrily. "You're really starting to piss me off, Jill. I thought we had everything ironed out and now you're kicking me out."

"That's what I'm doing alright. The only time I want to see you again is when you come by to get your things. Now, I've got stuff I need to do so goodbye. Oh, and congratulations on your big business deal. You're going to need the extra money. You can put it toward child support."

"What are you talking about! I've never heard you like this before. You're starting to scare me."

"And you're making me sick to my stomach so it's a fair trade off I'd say, now goodbye."

"Don't you dare hang up this phone before you tell me what the hell is going on. I deserve at least that much."

"You deserve plenty more than that, Brody, but I doubt you'll get everything you've got coming to you. But let's just say I've had my eyes opened. Your girlfriend dropped by today for a visit. Charming girl."

"That little bitch!"

"Now, Brody, that's not nice," Jill scolded sarcastically. "You know, I told her at first that I didn't believe a word she said, that I believed you over her. She told me things like she was the next Mrs. Sayer. That I basically dressed about as unsexy as a woman could get, and that I had no class. I was common. That you're going to seek full custody of Della when we get divorced, and she's looking forward to being a mother to our daughter. Ordinarily I wouldn't have been taken in at all by someone like her because she's a smooth one alright, but then she showed me the picture of you and her together. Cute couple! She even explained in sufficient detail how you two make love. Apparently the fire's been out at home for quite some time, I believe was how she said you put it, but that the two of you can't keep your hands off each other."

He groaned in disgust. "It's all a bunch of malarkey. I warned you she might not go away quietly. Look, Jill, I'm apologizing again from the bottom of my heart that I brought this into our lives, but you have to believe me. I never slept with that woman. The whole thing was exactly as I told you it was, and I swear to that on my dear mother's grave. I love you, babe."

"And I love you too, Brody, that's why this thing hurts so much. If I didn't care I probably wouldn't give it a second thought, but she's very convincing. Apparently you can't control yourself around anyone named Amanda."

She could tell he was really starting to get angry, although he was clearly struggling to hold his temper and keep his voice lowered. Offices had thin walls was all she could surmise. "So you'll take her word over mine, your own husband?"

"Pictures don't lie, Brody, and that was a doozy."

"Sometimes they do. It was probably photoshopped. Where did she have it?"

"On her phone, and it was you."

"How can you be sure?"

She told him about the shirt. "Women pay attention to stuff like that. So like I've already said, I've got to go. I'll also tell you again not to bother coming home tonight. I don't want you here, Brody. I can't make it any plainer than that. Goodbye."

She hung up the phone, thoroughly miserable. She and Brody had had fights before. Like every couple they sometimes found themselves at odds, but never like this. She was literally vibrating with fury, not sure how she'd managed to keep her voice as calm as she had when she'd felt like shouting at the top of her lungs.

The phone rang again, and she could see it was Brody but she refused to answer. Let him stew in his own juice for a while. As long as she lived she'd never get that picture out of her mind, them all cozied up together. For all his denials he certainly looked happy enough in that photo, and it was Amanda's hand resting proprietarily on his chest that stoked the flames. *Her* Brody. She wondered once again how understanding he would be if the situation were reversed and there was another man with his hands on her. It cut both ways.

The phone rang a couple of more times that evening and it was Brody both times, but strangely enough he didn't leave a message.

'What are you doing?' her conscience taunted her. 'You are purposefully driving him into the arms of another woman.'

"Oh shut up!" she yelled to an empty room and pounded the cushion beside her for at least three rounds. But aside from the tears she'd cried in the bathroom this afternoon, she remained dry-eyed, feeling hollow inside. She was tempted to pull all of his clothes off of their hangers, clean out the closet and heave everything that was his out into the front yard for him to pick up later. Rain or shine. But that was completely childish and other than providing entertainment for passersby and neighbours, it wouldn't accomplish anything other than venting her righteous anger. Besides, even wayward husbands had rights, and she could no more destroy his property than he would be permitted to destroy hers.

She glanced at the recliner. Just last night he'd sat in it and told her of his undying love. How she had wanted to believe him, *had* believed him. Maybe that's what hurt most of all. Being made a fool of. Come to think of it, she was as angry with herself as she was with him. She thought about Billy Redfern from university. Of course she hadn't loved him like she loved Brody now, but at the time she'd thought it was the real thing and had fallen hard. She told her mother and father about him, all her friends, and as the relationship deepened, wondered aloud when he'd put a ring on her finger. She'd been out with her friends one night and into the club walked Billy with another girl wrapped around him. They'd even kissed while they stood together at the bar.

She thought she would die from humiliation, and yes, she'd wanted to do murder that night too. She supposed that every woman had a Billy Redfern in their past, because that was what learning about love was like. There were highs and lows and bitter disappointments, especially when you really cared for someone. That was all part of the experience. Her heart had been broken that night at the club and she'd sworn she would never love again. And meant it. Then, six months later she'd met Brody and Billy Redfern seemed like a silly memory. And now Brody had found someone else. She guessed she must be pretty leave able based on her personal history. But when you were married to a man, shared a child and spent the past eight years together, that cut went so deep as to think it might never heal.

She didn't bother to put the deadbolts in place for the night. If Brody did decide he wanted to come home, she could hardly stop him. He was right. It was his home too. If he wanted to come in, a couple of deadbolts wouldn't stop him. He didn't get mad often, but he'd be good and angry now. She knew he would never harm her, he wasn't a violent man, but he was also someone not to be pushed too far either. If he came home, at whatever hour, and demanded to speak with her, she would have to deal with it.

It was after midnight when she turned out the lights and went to bed, but she wasn't tired in the least. So she got up and tried to watch a movie, but it didn't hold her interest. She was not a movie buff, nor did she have much interest in TV at all for that matter.

She'd sooner read a good book, but she couldn't think of anything that would distract her enough tonight to get her mind off the dismal state of her marriage. Nothing could accomplish that.

So she went back to bed and lay there wondering if Brody would come home as he'd threatened. It didn't seem so as the last time she looked at the clock it was 3:25. Finally, after tossing and turning, she felt sleep carrying her away.

Round black eyes were waiting for her, gleaming in the moonlight. They were not ordinary eyes. They were sinister in a way she'd never thought possible, so dark and distant they made her blood run cold. She backed up, but Wheelie came closer, those squeaky little wheels of his creaking ominously. He'd have made better time if he had all four wheels to support him in the chase, but he still made good progress on three as he nipped at her heels.

She turned to face the toy, his hot breath escaping from the hole that had once held his nose and mouth.

"Why won't you leave me alone?" he rasped in an unearthly voice that paralyzed her with fear. "You're staring at me, studying me as though I was some specimen, coming into my darkness as though you had a claim on my soul. You don't! And my name's not Wheelie! It's Punch Willigan!"

Jill backed up as fast as she could. "I ... I'm sorry."

"You're not sorry!" he screamed, now with a thousand voices. "You are a silly, stupid woman who does not understand — like those who confined me to a wall prison for eternity, although I was eventually freed. Just because *he* died doesn't mean that *I* should die too, and now I am confined once again. But these people are kind. You think you are so clever, but I know it's you when you climb those stairs. Each footfall is unique. Some walk much too slowly, some hurry through life, you're somewhere in between but you're just as unwelcome. You force your way into my world, but do not want to accept me into yours. Did you think you could just walk away? Leave my home without looking back and all the while with a plan to make a fool of me and my kind?" He rolled close enough now to lunge at her ankle, but she managed to pull her foot back in time, although he broke her skin during the attack. "No! It cannot be!"

Calling on all her ability as a former athlete, she pivoted on her heel and sprinted away to put distance between her and that dreadful toy. She ran fast and hard, her long legs covering the distance in ground-eating strides, her sneakers splashing through thick mud, sliding, slowing her down. Where had all the mud come from? It was almost impossible to make her way through it, although it didn't seem to bog the wheeled toy down. There was another nip on her ankle. Wheelie, or rather Punch Willigan, was directly behind her, sinking make belief teeth into her flesh. It really stung!

Off balance, she stumbled and that gave the toy the perfect advantage. He crashed into her with the gusto of wheels on fire. "You have disturbed me, and now so shall you be disturbed!" he raged.

"No! No! No!" she cried as she flailed under his attack. "You can't do this!"

She woke up, soaked with perspiration. Switching on the bedside lamp she sat up in bed, her back against the headboard. What a terrifying nightmare! It was bad enough thinking about that horrid little dog during broad daylight, having it showing up in her dreams was too much. She'd be glad when this project was finished, although she'd still go on the ghost tour she'd signed up for. That was low hanging fruit and it would be silly to pass it up. She might not believe in hauntings, ghosts and the like, but that didn't mean she didn't see value in the experience.

It was essential when working on a project to become immersed in it, whether that project was acting, writing, singing, dancing or whatever. You had to give one hundred percent of yourself, and to give it one hundred percent you had to *have* one hundred percent to give. She'd read that somewhere while studying to become a playwright. It might not be easy sometimes, but it was the only way. It would be the same with any discipline.

She recalled what her mother had said yesterday about documented cases of haunted toys. That surprised her, coming from her mother who she believed was as practical about these things as her daughter. Of more interest to Jill was what the actual explanation was, because there usually was one. She was not pliant, or in other words, easily convinced. Even in the face of overwhelming evidence, she stood her ground. That could be why she gave Brody so much leeway when another woman might have disbelieved him right out of the gate. She had, initially, but wasn't there always a chance that someone was telling the truth? The hard part was when you had one or in this case it seemed two practiced liars, although she'd never thought of Brody in that way. She still preferred not to. A good man had made a bad decision and it would be unwise to throw the baby out with the bathwater.

She picked up the book from the nightstand that she'd gotten into a few nights ago, before everything started going sideways. Back when she'd thought she was a happily married woman with a contented little girl. A mommy who believed that when she ordered something nice for her daughter online, that something nice would arrive. Also, she had not known at that point that Amanda even existed. Other than the company barbecue she hadn't been able to attend because Della was sick with an ear infection, there'd been no opportunity to fraternize with Brody's colleagues. Except for the Christmas party and she didn't recall seeing Amanda Leland at that event. Of course that was eight months ago, supposedly long before the affair started.

She opened the book and read a few lines, then reread them. When she'd gone over them for the third time to get the sense of what she was reading she realized it was going to be a wasted effort. So putting the novel back on the nightstand she switched off the lamp and got down under the covers again. She simply had to get more rest, because for sure she had to work on that play today.

Jill soon fell off to sleep and when she awakened again it was broad daylight. Scooting out of bed she checked the weather. Thankfully it was going to be much cooler today, with the threat of afternoon showers. At least that awful heat wave had passed and that was a relief. She might even go for a run this morning. Hmmm… She thought about it for a minute more before deciding that was precisely what she'd do. It was still early, only six fifteen, so traffic to either Summerside or Charlottetown hadn't really started yet. At least not in earnest.

It occurred to her that Brody might have come home while she was sleeping and bunked down in the spare room. There was no snoring, but she hurried down the hall to check anyway. The spare room was empty.

The bed hadn't been slept in since she'd made it from two nights ago. He had stayed away and that was the first time they'd ever spent the night apart in anger. Now it'd been two, but this was an entirely different set of circumstances and she still wondered if she'd made a rash decision. She could have let him come home and at least heard his side of the story, but it was a little late for that now.

She prided herself on being a good judge of character, Billy Redfern notwithstanding, and to her Brody had been honest about what had gone on with Amanda. It had the ring of truth to it, but so did some of the things Amanda had said. Jill sighed tiredly. Maybe her radar wasn't that foolproof after all. It came round to slap her in the face again that she had likely believed him only because she wanted to. Because she didn't want to lose him, and that would never work. Her eyes had been opened but good yesterday, especially with that photo. No matter what she believed or wanted to, she could never unsee the two of them together.

Now that she was calmed down enough to get some clarity with this thing, she was able to identify another very unsettling fact. Brody had been looking at Amanda with a smile she'd thought was reserved only for her. It was an intimate smile and he'd used it with another woman. She felt angry all over again. She really needed this run. Actually she could run from here to Ontario and back and her legs would give out long before this terrible ache inside of her was gone.

She pulled out a pair of short leggings, a sports bra and a fresh T from her dresser, tied her hair up in its customary ponytail and pulled it out the back opening of her peaked cap. She didn't bother with heart rate monitors or pedometers or any of that fancy smancy stuff. She wasn't preparing for a marathon today. This workout was for the soul, a keep from going crazy kind of run. The more analytical of the bunch would say it was symbolic, that she was trying to run away from her troubles. Bingo, because if she thought she could, she would, and if it weren't for Della, she'd never look back.

Headed to the bedroom to get socks, she was interrupted by the ringing of the telephone. Her first thought was that something had happened to Della. Grabbing the phone she didn't check the caller ID at the risk of losing the call. It was Brody.

She loved the sound of his voice, okay she craved it, already missing him and the hard part hadn't even begun yet.

"Jill," was all he said.

"What do you want, Brody?"

"I want to talk to you, why else would I have called. You sound as though you're in a hurry. Headed out somewhere? Nothing's wrong with Della is there?"

"Della's fine. I'm going out for a run. Try to clear my head."

"I'm coming home, Jill. I'm staying at a hotel in Summerside."

"Right," she said sarcastically.

"I can give you the room number and you can call back and check if you want. I suppose you'll think everything I say now is a lie."

"Pretty much. Besides what would calling prove? You're obviously not alone."

"I'm alone. I checked in alone and I'm still alone. I'm going down to check out and then I'm coming home. We're going to talk this thing out once and for all."

"I'm not sure I want to talk to you right now, Brody. I think what I need is to put some distance between us for a while. I don't want to make any decisions with the way I'm feeling right now."

He cleared his throat. "I respect that, but all I'm asking is that you listen to me before you go any further. Can you promise to do that?"

"I'm really not sure," she hedged. "Look, I'm not trying to play games but I don't even know which end is up right now. I'm still fighting to reach the surface."

"Jill, will you at least sit down with me and hear me out?"

"It seems to me I've already done that once."

"Alright, then let's do it again."

She sighed a sigh that came all the way up from her toes. Would she weaken when she saw him again, allow him to say things she desperately needed to hear? In that moment she knew she had to allow this to happen, of course she did, because whatever decisions she made now had to be in the best interests of their daughter.

"Okay fine, I'm going for a short run. If you get home before I do put some coffee on. I'll be up for a cup by the time I get back. I'll have a shower and then we can talk. But I'm not promising anything, Brody. The way I felt last night is the way I feel today, only with less sleep. At this point I'm not sure our marriage is salvageable since you're still actively cheating."

"Please, I know it looks bad, but stop rushing to judgment. It's not like you to do so. I'm going to go now and take a shower and then I'm driving home. I'll see you in about an hour I suppose by the time all is said and done."

"Fine, I'll be back as soon as I can," she said before ending the call.

Lacing up for the real thing, which is what she called an outdoor run, would do her good. She sometimes liked to listen to music. Something uplifting would be good this morning but cutting off her sense of hearing was negating a vital safety factor in place for her own protection, so she skipped the music.

She thought about that nightmare last night. It wasn't hard to piece together why, not with her spending so much time at Yeo House and staring at Wheelie. But that dream, a nightmare actually, had been so real. She shuddered.

Grabbing a pair of socks she headed for the back door where she kept her outdoor running shoes. She sat down to pull on the first sock, wincing in pain as she pulled it up over her ankle. Come to think of it she'd felt pain earlier this morning but had been too preoccupied to check it out. But she did now, and there was a small abrasion above her anklebone. Lifting her ankle up for closer inspection she could see that it went quite deep. Now how had she done that! She pulled her sock up over the wound and reached for her sneakers. Her eyes widened in surprise. They were covered in mud!

Chapter 13

Her mind shot back to the nightmare of a few hours ago. She'd dreamt that Wheelie had bitten her ankle, and that she'd been running through mud to get away from him. The mud on her sneakers looked fresh.

Then she remembered jumping out of bed when she'd dreamt that Della's teddy bear was in bed with her. She'd likely struck her ankle on the side of the bed in her haste, so that would explain the laceration. But the mud? Strange yes, but she must have left her sneakers outside and Brody had brought them in for her or something. It had rained a few days ago, so that was likely where the mud came from. There was a logical explanation for everything. But no, she thought, she'd gone for an inside run yesterday...

Knocking some of the mud off at the back door, she laced up and was soon on her way. She could feel tension begin to melt away as she drank in lungful's of fresh air, the scent of newly cut grass, the fragrance of people's flower gardens, the salty tang of the ocean. She heard birds singing and cars starting up as people prepared to leave for work. A brand new day, another fresh start, another chance to make things right. If that were only possible.

Foremost in her thoughts was Brody and the conversation she had agreed to a short time ago. That would be happening in about an hour and she wondered what her husband would have to say for himself this time. Would he talk his way out of it again? She had never had any reason to doubt his word prior to this, because he hadn't given her any. The reality of it was that once someone was caught in a lie, everything that came out of their mouth from that point onward was suspect.

But why did she automatically believe a stranger? Perhaps because Amanda had spoken to one of her worst fears, losing Brody. And it wasn't like the affair hadn't happened. He had admitted to it and she'd seen the photographic proof of them together, although that image would be considered tame compared to some cheating pictures. Did she still disbelieve him, or was she just furious at his betrayal? How would she expect Brody to behave if she was the one who needed forgiving? How would she feel if Brody refused to listen, to believe her, or not forgive her. Be turned away by the man she thought loved her. That she wasn't worthy of his forgiveness. These were agonizing thoughts, all of them. wanted to believe his version of events, wanted desperately for this nightmare to be over, but what could he possibly say now to save himself?

With a concerted effort she put it out of her mind, again, and thought about the ghost tour set for tomorrow night at Yeo House. She smiled. Anyone who knew her would laugh at the idea of her going on another ghost tour, but here she was signed up. She'd no doubt get a kick out of it, as she had the others, which was probably why everyone else was going too. Some people enjoyed being scared, that's why the horror industry was so lucrative.

Heading back, she was a kilometre from home when Brody passed by with a wave. Good, that meant he'd have the coffee ready by the time she got there and grabbed a shower. She'd need a good stiff black cup of coffee to get through what promised to be another difficult session.

She slowed her pace, finishing the last few hundred metres at a walk to cool down. Kicking off her shoes at the back door she stopped to inhale the tantalizing aroma of freshly brewed coffee before grabbing clean clothes from the bedroom. She stepped into the kitchen to tell him she'd only be a few minutes.

"I'll meet you in the living room," she said. "I think we might be more comfortable there."

"Jill! What happened to your ankle? Your sock's all bloody. Did you cut it while you were running? It's bleeding pretty good."

"Oh that. I think I struck it on the bedpost getting out of bed the other morning. It's nothing."

Sitting down he patted his knee. "Here, put your foot up. I'll take a look at it. It'd have to be quite deep to bleed like that."

"It's nothing, really."

He reached for her foot and she reluctantly raised it into his hands. Peeling the sock off he inspected it closely. "You say you hit it on the bedpost?"

"I must have. I honestly don't recall doing it, but that's the only thing that comes to mind. You say it's cut? I thought I'd only knocked the skin off."

He looked at it again, closely. "From what I can see it looks like puncture wounds. It's almost as if you were bitten, but I'm sure you'd remember something like that. There's antiseptic cream in the medicine chest, put some of that on it and a Band-aid so it won't get infected."

Her mind raced back to the nightmare. That was the only biting incident she could think of, but it had only been a dream. She'd figure it out though. She'd struck her ankle on something sharp and given her stressed-out mental state lately it was little wonder she couldn't recall it.

"Okay, that's what I'll do. However it happened, running must have aggravated it. Now I'm all sweaty so I'll go take that shower and be right back for some coffee."

The touch of Brody's hand on her foot felt like a caress. She still wanted him. Badly. Being angry with someone didn't mean you stopped loving them, desiring them. The sound of his voice, the low sexy rumble, had the same powerful effect. And now there was an excellent chance he would soon belong to someone else. If their talk failed this morning, how could it be any other way? She had more self-respect than to take second place to another woman. She knew women who'd been in similar circumstances and made peace with the fact that their husband had a mistress. It meant they didn't have to alter their lifestyle, but she had to have all of her husband — or nothing. Whatever was left after the fallout they'd always be co-parents to Della, and so for her sake their relationship had to remain amicable.

Later she joined Brody in the living room where he'd set a large mug of coffee on the end table for her before settling into the recliner. He looked as though he hadn't slept much last night either.

"I made hazel nut," he told her.

She drank deeply from the mug before setting it back down. "I know. I could smell it outside as I was walking up to the house."

"That's your favourite, isn't it?"

"You know it is. Stop it, Brody."

"Stop what? I thought you'd like it so that's what I made, or did I get that wrong too?"

"I mean stop trying to butter me up. This is hard enough as it is. Besides, you trying to kiss up is only going to make me madder."

He puffed a long tired sigh. "I only asked you to keep an open mind."

Jill shrugged. "My mind is as open as it can possibly be under the circumstances. I mean you're still walking around breathing."

He took a swig of coffee himself then set the cup aside. "That sounds ominous."

She swallowed a flash of irritation. "Honestly, Brody, how do you expect me to feel? I went to bed two nights ago thinking I had a great marriage. I loved my husband and I thought he loved me. And then out of the blue I don't have such a great marriage anymore because you invited a bimbo into it and now naturally she thinks she's got a claim on you. So yes, I'm having a bit of a difficult time processing all of this. And just when I think we've got everything talked out, and I've apologized for making you feel left out, and you apologized for looking elsewhere because of that and assured me it was over, boom! It blows up in my face again. How do you think I should feel? How should I be handling all of this? Please tell me."

"For one thing you could trust me. I know. I betrayed that trust when I became involved with Amanda, or I should say started paying her more attention than she deserved. I've already apologized for that and unless my memory is completely failing me, you said you forgave me. And now we're back at square one because of that visit."

Jill took another long drink of coffee, fortification for what amounted to the fight of her life. Were there more truths to be told? This may be the last conversation they had before they separated. If he finally found it in his heart to come clean and corroborate what Amanda had told her, that it was indeed an ongoing affair, she would have no alternative but to either seek a trial separation or file for divorce.

Divorce was the last thing she wanted. She didn't want to lose the man she still loved with every fibre of her being. She didn't want Della to have to deal with a broken home. Neither did she want to teach her daughter it was okay for a man to treat her badly, and still stay with him. It had been said a million times that couples stayed together for the children, but if that meant animosity and discord, then Della would indeed be better off with her mother and father living apart.

And maybe at the end of the day Brody would divorce her in favour of Amanda. It could go in any number of directions and she steeled herself to continue, deciding to fight fire with fire.

"Yes, because of that visit," she answered him. "First let me ask you this, Brody. You said you never slept with Amanda, but if it wasn't sexual, why do you keep referring to it as an affair?"

"Guilt I guess. I knew what I was doing was wrong and it *felt* like I was having an affair on you. But no, it was never sexual."

She folded her arms across her chest. "Okay, I'm going to ask you this flat out, and please, don't dance around. Not anymore. It's a yes or no question and I want you to answer me honestly. No matter what my feelings are, or the future is for us or whatever, can you promise me you'll do that? Not tell me what you think I want to hear, but answer honestly the first time?"

His jaw set, he crossed his legs and knit his hands together in his lap. "Fire away, Jill."

"Do you want a divorce?"

He did not hesitate. "Why, so I can marry Amanda?"

The pain in her stomach was back. "That would be the general idea, so do you? Yes or no!"

"No! Of course I don't want a divorce. Don't be ridiculous! I don't know why you believed all that crap she told you."

"Well, Brody, she's a beautiful woman and I can certainly see why she would turn your head. I don't want to go over all that again, I mean why she happened to turn yours, but where we are now is what the real truth is. She was very convincing. So either you're a better liar than I gave you credit for or she is an outstanding actress, but one of you is not telling me the truth. And I'm the fool in the middle trying to sort this mess out."

He looked as though he was trying to hold onto his temper, and succeeded in doing so as he spoke calmly. "I would have thought that I'd have the edge. I've never lied to you before, Jill. I've always told you the truth."

"Until Amanda came along."

"Yes, alright, until Amanda came along. I keep apologizing for that terrible error in judgment, but I guess in vain. I know I hurt you. I will go to my grave understanding that. I can only imagine what it would feel like if you'd done that to me. I'm sorry. I am, more than I can possibly ever explain. I don't know what else I can do besides apologize."

"Amanda called you a player. Said she knew there'd been other women before her."

"And when would that have been? Hmmm? All I ever do is work. But if you think I can juggle half a dozen women and a marriage and a demanding career, then I guess I should be flattered. In actual fact I only ever strayed once, with Amanda, and I've sworn to you on my mother's grave that I've never slept with her. I was tempted, I've admitted to that, but I couldn't go through with it. I planned to tell you all about this once I'd walked away and was fully clear of it, but that's not the way it played out."

"And your administrative assistant, Amanda, I don't know what her last name was. Tell me about her."

"Amanda Vickers? She worked for me for a while when I first went with the firm until her husband got transferred to Toronto. What about her?"

"Amanda Leland said you'd had an affair with her and gotten her pregnant, that she left town because of you."

He threw back his head and laughed out loud. "She told you that. And you believed her. Come on, Jill. You know better than that."

Jill drained her mug then sat back pensively. "I so wish you hadn't had that weak moment ... moments. I can't get that picture of the two of you out of my mind. Her hand on your chest, so proprietary. And she's very beautiful. Don't get me wrong, I have plenty of self-respect, but I know I can't compare to her in the looks department. I run a very distant fourth or fifth at best. She said she felt sorry for you that you had to look at the likes of me everyday."

Fire danced in his eyes. "Don't you ever let me hear you say something like that again! You are a beautiful woman. No scratch that, you're gorgeous! Those long sexy legs, your pretty hair and those eyes of yours are incredible. What more do you want? I remember when I started going out with you way back when, all the guys were jealous. You were a catch and I've never been sorry I was the one who caught you. That was my lucky day.

"They say guys aren't romantic, and I don't claim to be any Romeo, but I remember the night I asked you to marry me. My stomach was in knots, and later, after I got home alone, I felt like bawling with relief. I had this fear you were going to turn me down. I've never told you that but since we're telling truths, there it is."

Jill sniffed. She'd never heard that story before and it made her love him more, or more properly reinforced the love she already felt. "One thing I loved was that special way you smiled when you looked at me, Brody. That look was for me, your wife. That's the smile I saw you giving Amanda in that picture, and it broke my heart. It took the ground right out from under me, although I didn't let on to her."

"I'm sorry," he said. "It's just a smile but let me tell you something. I have never, at any moment since we've been together, felt about her or anyone else the way I feel about you. That picture was taken when she first started flirting with me. It was the company barbecue. Everyone was kidding around and then suddenly I find myself in this selfie and I went along with it, like a fool. I actually forgot all about it.

"Maybe it's because I was angry about you being too busy to be with me, I don't know. You've apologized for that and I've accepted it, but tell me, what can I do, other than apologize, to make things right between us?"

Jill hugged herself, chilled in spite of the hot coffee. "I want it to never have happened, that never would you have given another woman that special kind of attention. But of course it did happen and now I want those terrible memories to go away. I want to be able to believe every word out of your mouth, like I used to. I want my trust in you to be as strong as it was before all of this came to light. I want things to be like they were before, and that there will never be another Amanda Leland marching into our lives like she had a right to be there. I don't want to share you, Brody, and I never will. That's what I want, but your question was how you can make it happen. How you can make all of this right and put our marriage back on the rails.

"It's a terrible feeling to find out you never really knew the person you loved. If someone had asked me even two weeks ago if this could happen to us, I'd have laughed and said never! But things do happen and I really don't know how I can get past this. I keep asking for your word, your honesty. You keep saying that's what you're telling me and just when you have me convinced, along comes the other party telling me the opposite is true."

He scrubbed his face tiredly. "I was afraid something like that would happen, but it does surprise me she would go that far. Don't get me wrong. I'm not trying to shift the blame onto her. I was a willing participant, but never to the extent she's making it out to be. What I want, and what I probably don't deserve, is for you to believe in me enough to tell me you accept what I'm telling you is the truth. You might feel I haven't earned back that right, but before we go one step further that's a question I need to have you answer for me. Can I ask for your trust that I'm telling you the truth about this?"

Jill dabbed at her eyes, staring at the empty coffee mug. Could she do it? Could she find it within herself to believe what her husband was telling her? Start trusting him again? Maybe trust *could* be rebuilt and they could put this whole thing behind them. Her next words had to be carefully chosen, because what she said could help close this chasm between them.

She looked her husband straight in the eye. "Is it over between you and Amanda?"

He leaned forward as though for emphasis. "Yes, it is, and it was never to the extent that she told you it was. Do you believe me?"

She desperately wanted to. So much was riding on her answer. "Okay, Brody, I believe you. What you can do, is live up to that."

Closing his eyes he released a pent-up sigh of what sounded like relief. "Thank you, Jill, for believing me — and I will. Now, I have something I want to show you."

He reached in his shirt pocket and pulled out his cellphone. "I should say I have something I want you to hear."

Activating the device, he laid it on the table between them. The recording began with a conversation that was already in progress.

Amanda's voice came through as clear as a bell. "Brody, I'm in love with you and I know with time I can convince you that you love me too. I don't want to lose you."

And then Brody spoke. "Amanda I've told you this before and I'm saying it again and I want you to listen. I am not in love with you. I am in love with my wife. All you and I ever had between us was flirtation, a couple of kisses, and that was wrong. You know we never slept together. I paid you way more attention than I should have and I apologize for that. It was never my intention to lead you on."

"So what was going on with your wife?"

"That's none of your business. What is my business is that you went to my home and spoke with my wife, told her a bunch of lies. That I was a player and you were only one of the many women I've been with. That is untrue. I am a happily married man who got off track. Once. That's all. Even the friendship we had was wrong because I knew all along you wanted more. I was enjoying your attention, but it's over."

"Brody, don't you see? Your wife believed what I told her. She didn't at first but when I showed her the picture of us together she did. So the heavy lifting is done. I've taken care of it. You just have to do the leaving. It's true we have never made love, but we will when you're ready. I'm sorry if I made you feel rushed. We could be good together, you and me."

"Amanda, I want you to walk away from this and not look back. I'm married and I'm not going to leave my wife. Ever."

"But that's my point. You think you're happy but being married to me would be so much better. For one thing you'd be rich. When my grandfather passes away I will inherit his estate and as you know, it's substantial. I want you, Brody."

"This stops here, tonight, and furthermore if you go near my family again I'll take action against you. I'll involve the police and I know you wouldn't want that black mark against your name."

Amanda laughed, and Jill remembered the patronizing sound. "Don't threaten me. It would be your word against mine, that it was you who behaved inappropriately."

"You might want to rethink that, Amanda. I'm recording you." Jill could hear the sound of his finger tapping his shirt pocket. "Now like I said, walk away and leave me and my family alone. I mean it! We will be polite to each other here at work, but that's the extent of it. It's over. Close the door on your way out please."

Jill could hear the sound of someone weeping. "I hate you, Brody Sayer. I don't know how I could have ever thought I loved you or wanted you. I take it back. You're a genuine bastard and your wife is welcome to you. Goodbye."

There was the sound of a door closing much too loudly, and then the recording ended.

Brody reached ahead and deactivated his cellphone. "There it is. I screwed everything up so badly I knew I needed proof, so that's what I did last night. Not at the hotel," he stressed, "but at the office after the meeting. I've been trying to extricate myself from this for a while and I'm glad it's over. Thank you for taking the chance and believing me, Jill. If this goes toward winning your trust back, then I am a happy man. I will try to think of a way to make this all up to you. I've put you through hell and I'm sorry. It will never happen again."

He went to the sofa where Jill sat crying, cradling her in his arms.

Brody's cellphone rang and he grabbed it. "Yes, Don, I had some personal business to attend to this morning. I'll be there within the hour."

"I take it that was Don Sommers," she said after he ended the call.

"The one and only, so I've got to run. I love you, Jill, and I've got that bottle of champagne in my car from last night. We'll drink a toast to our company's success when

I get home. In the meantime, remember how much I love you."

In minutes he'd changed his clothes and left for the office.

He had no sooner backed out of the driveway than she heard a commotion in Della's room. What on earth! Running down the hall she flung open the door. What she saw stopped her cold.

Chapter 14

The room was in chaos, toys that had been stored away in the toy box were now thrown about the room in total disarray. Her eyes flew to Della's chalkboard sitting atop her desk. PLAYTIME had been printed in the same block letters as before in green chalk. She stepped further into the room unsure of what to make of what she saw. Nothing was moving now, although everything had certainly been displaced.

Without warning the bedroom door slammed shut behind her, startling her. The room grew dim despite the mid-morning sunshine that had begun to sneak around the window blinds in defiance of the dismal forecast. Suddenly her attention was drawn to the chalkboard again. The previous message had somehow been erased, and a new one was in the process of being printed by an unseen hand. She watched, stunned, until all of the letters appeared in pink. TREPIDO

Jill remembered her Latin lessons. She had studied the ancient language with a view to improving her vocabulary and hoping it would serve as a springboard when she found the time to learn other Romance languages. She was already functionally bilingual in French, but thought she'd like to give Spanish a try. She looked at the board again. She understood the message: BE AFRAID

A strange energy filled the room. Someone was watching her. She had to get out of here. Now! She hurried for the door. It wouldn't budge. The doorknob would not turn and try as she might she could not get the door open. What was going on! And after Brody left too, which meant there was no one to help dislodge this thing. Her cellphone was on the charger in the kitchen. Perfect! She was stuck in this room and she wasn't about to start yelling for help. The neighbours would think she'd lost her mind. She tried the door again, but it was frozen in place.

Okay. She'd be a little hungry by the time Brody got home, hopefully by six o'clock, but it was reassuring to know the cavalry was only a few hours away.

Suddenly she felt as though she couldn't breathe, it was like the weight of a rhinoceros sitting on her chest. It was as though every bit of oxygen was being sucked out of the room. Hurrying to the window she clawed to release the catch, but it held fast. She could feel herself becoming lightheaded, about to faint. Turning she looked for something to smash the glass, and then as abruptly as it had begun, her breathlessness disappeared.

She could breathe freely, the pressure against her chest easing.

Behind her she could hear the bedroom door opening and she made a dash toward it, only to have it slam shut in her face. Any closer and it would have struck her. She jumped back in alarm, but the door opened again, standing temptingly ajar a foot or so away. She lunged for the opening only to have it close with a resounding crash a second time, again narrowly missing her.

She looked wildly around the room for something to throw into the path of the door so she could escape should it reopen. Nothing came to hand. She spied a large stuffed giraffe lying upside down in the corner. That would work, but it was as though it weighed a thousand pounds. She couldn't budge it. The chalkboard! That was sturdy enough to do the job. Good plan! Turning back toward the desk to grab hold of it she saw there was a new message printed in yellow: HA HA HA

Jill could hear her cellphone ringing in the kitchen. Probably Jack confirming their coffee date this afternoon. She'd miss the meeting because she'd become a prisoner in her daughter's bedroom. If she was the type to be easily intimidated she'd be in hysterics by now, but she knew she had to keep her head for what might happen next. It seemed anything was possible. She looked at the chalkboard where an even more ominous message was now printed: I'M COMING FOR YOU

"Good!" she shouted, breathing hard. She was darn good and angry now. "You come for me, whoever you are or whatever you are. Come! I welcome you! But I must warn you, I don't believe in any of this hocus pocus stuff so your time and energy is being wasted trying to scare me. I invite you to do your worst! I can't stop you anyway. Come on! Let's see what you've got! You think I'm scared of a locked door and a little bit of chalk! Ha! You don't know me very well."

Silence. Nothing stirred in the room. "Can't you hear me!" she yelled. "I don't believe in ghosts or whatever else is going on here, so either step up or go haunt someone else. You're wasting my time! I'm busy."

Nothing, although the door was still closed. "What's the matter! Is this the best you've got? I thought ghosts were supposed to have all these things covered. You've been trying to spook me for days but guess what, it's not working!" she continued to shout bravely. "You're not much of a ghost if this is all you can come up with. This is kiddy school! If I had the time to waste I could figure this all out in a heartbeat. Figure you out. You might be fooling other people, buddy," she yelled, "but you're not fooling me."

It was as if the air around her instantly became supercharged, but still she stood, shoulders thrown back, challenging her unseen foe. Ready to do battle. All at once she felt inordinately tired, as though she couldn't keep her eyes open. She became ragdoll limp. Dropping helplessly onto the bed she fell into a deep sleep.

She awoke feeling refreshed, but oh the dream she'd had. Whew! Actually, another nightmare. It was one of those situations where the more you came awake the more grateful you were that it hadn't been real. She'd be glad when the project was over. These unsettling dreams were beginning to become tiresome. And why was she sleeping in Della's room? Perplexed she swung her legs over the side of the bed, still blinking the sleep from her eyes. Boy that dream had been something else. She looked around the room. Everything was in place. The chalkboard sitting atop the desk had been erased clean, the chalk waiting in readiness for Della when she returned home. Yep, it had only been a dream.

The time! My goodness! It must be late and she had to get on the road to Charlottetown or Jack would think she wasn't coming. She'd hoped to put some time in on the play before she left but that wouldn't be possible now. Brody had teased her about working with Jack Rinsky. It's the perfect play combination her husband had laughed — Jack and Jill. But what was going on here was far from a fairy tale.

She couldn't believe her eyes when she looked at the clock in the kitchen. It was 9:30

a.m. Why that was the exact time Brody had left for the office. What! Never mind she told herself, it meant she still had plenty of time before she had to leave for Charlottetown. There was a message on her cellphone. Jack had called to confirm coffee, so she'd call him back, but first she wanted to speak to her mother and see how Della was getting along. Find out if there had been any more sleep disruptions. She also wanted to speak to her daughter. She missed her.

Typically the conversation didn't last long because Della wanted to get back to her dolls. There was no mention of Bear Boy, and she mentally crossed her fingers.

"I love you, Mommy," Della said in her sweet little voice before telling her mother goodbye.

Jill felt lighthearted when she thought about Brody and the final resolution of the Amanda thing. Now they could finally put all of that behind them and move on. She had made the difficult decision to believe him, trust him, and she'd forever be grateful for that leap of faith. He'd been telling the truth all along, and it helped to right her world. She couldn't imagine that woman would make a second appearance in her life. There'd be no good reason for it. If someone had dressed her down the way Brody had done to Amanda, she wouldn't want to have anything more to do with them.

Okay, she thought as she made her way into her office, she had to get to work. First she'd see if she could find any more interesting tidbits on the Yeo family, although from what she'd discovered so far, there were many Yeos who had immigrated to Canada from the south of England in about the same time period as James Yeo Sr. Something interesting she noticed on an online site dedicated to his history, was that his second-born child with his first wife, Mary, was a boy whom they'd named James. It was noted the child only survived until the age of two. Following the death of Mary, James Yeo Sr. remarried and apparently determined to have a surviving namesake, also named one of his seven children, James Yeo Jr.

She continued to scroll, caught up in the story. Once they were in in PEI, as Prince Edward Island is most commonly known, the James Yeo Sr. family settled in what was called at the time Porthill. It was common in those days for the name of a new place to be named after an old place in the former homeland. In this case the original Porthill was in Devon, England. It wasn't until 1964 that the community's name in Prince Edward Island was changed to its present designation of Port Hill located in Prince County, PEI.

She scanned old diaries in general, especially those from the Maritime provinces of which Prince Edward Island was part. It seemed in the mid to late 1800's, the time frame she was interested in, people were much more socially active. And of course the Yeo's, being prominent, wealthy members of Prince Edward Island society, almost certainly would have entertained a great deal.

That would have made for a busy kitchen as it was expected by British custom that callers be served tea. If they followed the traditional tea served back in England, in addition to the hot beverage there would have been delicate sandwiches, cakes and pastries and likely scones with clotted cream. She remembered the inviting parlour at Yeo House laid out for this daily refreshment. Whatever the menu, kitchen staff would have been kept hard at work baking any number of confections and if there were gatherings of any size, that demand would increase tenfold. She could imagine the tempting aroma of almost constant baking during daylight hours.

Add to those employee's responsibilities the care of a house the size of the mansion, as it was regarded in those times. Servants would have seen to the needs of perhaps a family of twelve at one point, if any of the elder children from the first marriage had not left yet to make their own way. That would include sizeable meal preparation, aside from the baking, in what we would now consider a relatively modest workspace, given the size of the kitchen itself and the pantry, and with no modern conveniences. If there was an angry ghost in the mansion, she chuckled to herself, it may be that of an overworked servant.

And what would it have been like to be a child in that busy household? She was sure those children would have been aware of their status in the community, luxury earned by the father and bestowed upon succeeding family members. However she could find no evidence to suggest that James Yeo Sr.'s sons relied solely on the advantages of their father's success.

She yawned as she left her search sites and closed the laptop. It was fun to take a step back in time and revisit the lives of those who'd long ago left this earth for either punishment or reward, but she was only too happy to enjoy the conveniences of the twenty-first century. She thought about the high temperatures they'd experienced yesterday. It was unusual to get that hot here on the Island, but when it did those Victorian-era women were still bound by convention to wear long heavy skirts and a mountain of underclothing. Long-sleeved bodices on those kitchen dresses must have been suffocating. And even the gentry, while making social calls or attending any kind of a special function, wore attire that would have been equally as burdensome, just fancier. There'd also be an extravagantly adorned platter of a hat pinned atop their head too. No thanks, give her today's shorts and tank tops.

She thought about James Yeo Jr.'s time in the mansion. He'd had it built when he was thirty-eight years of age and was able to enjoy the grand old home for fifty-one years until his death in 1916.

And what of his family? The walls that had echoed with the ring of children's laughter had no doubt wept with sorrow too. Money did not spare anyone the hardships of life. Everyone was on equal footing when it came to the unpredictability of human experience.

Glancing at the clock she saw it was time to start getting ready to go meet with Jack in Charlottetown, and she thought yet again what a godsend he was for her playwriting career. Not that she didn't do other types of writing, but plays had become her professional focus. Maybe after Ghosts in the House? had been written and staged she'd concentrate on drama, although she tended to be more inclined toward comedy and she'd enjoyed encouraging success in that regard.

Quickly changing into cotton slacks, a loose-fitting blouse and sandals, she pinned her hair up on top of her head and applied a dab of lip gloss before hurrying to the kitchen to pick up her car keys. Not one to misplace things, she religiously hung her keys on the peg by the back door as soon as she got home. But her keys were not where they should have been. Great, she was going to be late because she had no clue where else they could be. Jack was a nice guy and would understand, but it was rude to keep people waiting and for such a silly thing as misplaced car keys. Unfortunately she only had one set. Brody had lost the spare when he'd borrowed her car while his was in for a tire change. She'd meant to order a replacement but hadn't gotten around to it yet.

"Come on, Jill, think," she said aloud. "They've got to be here somewhere."

She retraced her steps in her mind after coming home yesterday. Ahh let's see, Amanda had been waiting for her on the verandah and that had thrown her off. She'd been more than a little upset after the woman's visit, so she'd likely shoved her keys in her purse without thinking. She checked. They weren't there.

"Come on!" she all but shouted as though that would somehow produce results. She remembered the pocket of her shorts. Yes, that's where they were. The pockets were empty.

Was this another strange occurrence? So far she'd been able to explain almost everything away, except for the face at the window, but now her keys had disappeared. She'd sound like a ninny having to call Jack and cancel because of something like this.

She'd already looked in the same places at least three times, but where else was there to check? She went around to the front of the house again, but there were no keys on either the chairs or the table holding the large clay pot of red geraniums. Then she saw something shiny. Her keys were sitting on the surface of the potting soil. She didn't recall putting them there, but she'd been distracted. The pot had a wide lip so she'd likely set them down and they'd slipped over the edge.

"There," she announced triumphantly. "Mystery solved."

Grabbing the keys she climbed into her car, but it wouldn't start. Brody had told her about experiencing the same thing with his vehicle. There was no logical reason why hers wouldn't turn over either. She'd fuelled up yesterday and had recently had the oil changed along with the regular maintenance. The car was not yet two years old, so it couldn't be a battery issue. It had been working perfectly when she'd parked it yesterday. She tried it again. Nothing.

"Having trouble, Mrs. Sayer?" their neighbour Ronnie Thurlowe asked as he walked across the yard to her car. "I came out to cut the grass and it looked like something might be wrong with your vehicle. Mind if I take a look?"

Jill put down her window. "It won't start and I'd love it if you could take a look. Are you on vacation?"

"Yes. Bonnie and I are doing day trips this year, but today we're relaxing at home. We're going over to New Brunswick tomorrow to see our daughter, Sandra and her husband, and our grandchildren. Okay, try it for me."

She did so.

"Hear that clicking?" he asked. "I'd say it's your battery for sure. Give me a minute and I'll give you a boost, but I'd get that checked if I were you. You don't want to end up stranded somewhere, especially at night."

It didn't take long for the older man to have her car up and running and Jill thanked him profusely for his help before backing out of the driveway and hurrying away. She'd call Jack along the way to tell him she was going to be a little late. Everyone had car problems from time to time. She was sure he'd understand.

She tried to reach him several times as she hurried through the beautiful PEI countryside to the Trans Canada Highway that would take her to Charlottetown. Jack wasn't answering and not surprisingly his mailbox was full. He was not a slave to modern technology. Sometimes he bothered with his cellphone and sometimes he didn't, preferring to rely on his old school landline. Such was obviously the case today and she could picture him sitting in the coffee shop looking at his watch. He was a busy man, despite the fact that it was summertime. As he liked to put it, the arts never take a vacation. Jack was up to his eyeballs in commitments to the arts and loving every minute of it. She was grateful he took as much time as he did to mentor her, and she couldn't imagine he'd be amused if he thought she wasn't taking that privilege seriously enough.

After what seemed like far too long she finally made it to the highway. Now she'd make better time, although she wasn't one to speed … well by much anyway. She enjoyed a perfect driving record and had no intention of compromising it today just so she wouldn't be late for a meeting. It was a very important meeting, but nevertheless…

Slipping into the inside lane she let her speedometer creep up past the posted ninety kilometre per hour limit, to a hundred. Normally she didn't like doing that, but she was in a hurry. And then she could feel the accelerator being pressed down under her foot as the car steadily gained speed, only she hadn't increased the pressure on the pedal. What was going on with this car? Holding onto the steering wheel tightly she saw she had climbed to one hundred and twenty, not exactly racetrack speed, but it was thirty kilometres over the posted limit. She took her foot off the accelerator altogether, but the car notched up another five kilometres on a flat stretch.

Quickly coming up on a slower moving car she had no alternative than to swing into the passing lane and overtake the vehicle ahead of her. It was the same with the next vehicle and the next as her car continued to accelerate. She was in a runaway car hurtling through traffic and scared out of her wits. No matter how many times she depressed the brake pedal it made no difference in her speed. She was flying.

In desperation she pushed as hard as she could on the brake pedal, but still nothing as the speedometer climbed to one hundred and thirty. The accelerator must be stuck, but when she touched it tentatively with her foot she could feel it wasn't down at all now. It had returned to its original position. None of this made any sense at all.

Was this thing going to continue to go faster? Was she going to get in a wreck, possibly kill some innocent motorist? Or be killed herself? She gripped the steering wheel as though it was a lifeline, never more terrified in her life. She desperately wanted to call for help but feared becoming distracted would only make matters worse. She had to stay in full control of this automobile. There was the chance that the computer could right itself and lose speed, but it was a slim hope at best. She knew zip about cars, but it had to be something malfunctioning in the electronic system that controlled the throttle causing it to accelerate. Her speed jumped yet again.

"Please, God!" she prayed. "Help me!"

And then she saw that traffic up ahead had slowed, was bunching up in a sea of brake lights as her own vehicle went even faster, barreling toward the traffic jam.

Chapter 15

It couldn't be more than a quarter of a kilometre away, just two hundred and fifty metres — not even three hundred yards. Then she heard the siren, saw the red and blue flashing lights reflected in her rear view mirror. The police must be on their way to an accident up ahead and she knew she must pull over, but she couldn't, not as this speed. And then miraculously her car began to decelerate, rapidly losing momentum and she hadn't touched the brake pedal. She rolled to a stop on the shoulder of the road, while up ahead, whatever had slowed the vehicles down had apparently been resolved. Traffic now appeared to be moving along at a normal pace. The police were pulling *her* over, and not much wonder. She had been speeding, big time!

She'd seen enough television shows to know that anyone being intercepted by police was required to remain in their vehicle, so she did. The officer sat in the cruiser and when she looked in her rear-view mirror she could see the radio receiver in his hand. No doubt he was calling in her license plate to see if there were any warrants out on her. For all that police officer knew she could be an escaped murderer.

Finally the slow walk up began, and she saw him touch the back of her car with his thumb. Leave a print to record that he had stopped this vehicle.

He would either be friendly, or he wouldn't. He wasn't. "License and registration please," he said.

She had both of them ready, passing him the leather case that contained them.

"Take them out please."

She withdrew both documents and did as she was told. Taking them he read her name. "Do you know why I'm stopping you?" he asked her.

"To help me, I assume."

"Help you? What's going on today?"

"My car started to go really fast and I couldn't slow it down. I was so scared."

His expression clearly said he didn't believe her. "When you saw me behind you, you slowed down and pulled over. There didn't seem to be any mechanical problem with your car then. Where are you headed?"

"Into Charlottetown for a meeting, for which I'm hopelessly late."

She knew as soon as the words were out of her mouth she had hung herself. Of course he'd think that because she was late for a meeting she'd been treading rubber to try to make it on time. Her goose was cooked and she'd get a really hefty fine out of this. She might even lose points. So much for a perfect driving record.

"Do you know how fast you were going?"

"Too fast."

"You were going 140 in a ninety. Do you know what can happen at the speed you were going if you had an accident on this busy highway?"

"I'm sorry, but I am telling you the truth about my car accelerating on its own. I was practically standing on the brake and it had no affect at all. It was terrifying. Please believe me."

He plainly didn't. After all he'd witnessed her travelling at a high rate of speed, weaving in and out of traffic, and then when he'd activated his lights and siren, she was able to pull over as pretty as you please. Whatever had gone wrong with the car seemed to have righted itself as quickly as it had malfunctioned.

"I'll be right back," he said before returning to his vehicle with her license and registration. More time passed.

Her cellphone rang. Jack. "It's not nice to stand up the director of your play," he said trying to inject levity into his voice, but she could also hear the annoyance. "I take it you're not coming."

She told him about the series of mishaps that had made her miss the meeting and that she had tried to contact him several times. "I'm so sorry, Jack," she told him, "but I won't be coming today. I've got to get this car

245

checked out before I go any further. I'm sitting here right now on the side of the highway waiting for a police officer to write me up a ticket, a really big one I assume, and it's not even my fault. But I haven't got a leg to stand on."

"I'm glad you're alright and that you didn't have an accident. We'll try for tomorrow, same time. I'll keep my cell with me and if you can't make it, let me know. Ciao, and be careful."

She was surprised when the constable, despite his unfriendly demeanour, gave her a break by knocking her speed down a little, but it was still going to be expensive. She signed her name as requested and took her copy. She felt sick to her stomach.

"Now," she said, "would you mind calling a tow truck for me? My accelerator was stuck like I told you it was. For some reason it got unstuck as you were pulling me over, but this thing was out of control and I've never been more terrified in my life. I thought I was either going to kill someone or be killed myself ... or both. Please tell them I want it taken to MacTavishes in Summerside, and that I'll need a drive back there myself in the truck. My husband can pick me up after work."

He studied her. "You're saying the accelerator was stuck."

"Yes, it took off on its own. I was driving along just fine and then it started to go faster and faster. It could be something to do with the computer system, you know, the throttle. It was as though this car had a mind of its own."

He nodded, thawing marginally. "Okay, I'll call roadside assistance for you and I tell you what. If when you have the car checked there is a problem with the acceleration system, then get that in writing from the dealership and I'll rescind the ticket. Call me," he said, passing her one of his business cards.

She thanked him. He wasn't such a bad guy after all. He'd given her a break on the ticket and now he was offering to tear it up when she found out what was wrong with the car. He couldn't be any fairer than that.

It was a slow day at the dealership and they were able to take her car in right away. She explained in detail what had happened, the unexpected acceleration, and how she'd been at the mercy of the malfunctioning vehicle. She also told the service manager about the dead battery.

She hadn't had any problems with it at all until today, and then boy had it made up for lost time.

While she was waiting she called Brody and left a message, and he called right back. He was aghast when she told him about her experience on the highway.

"It seemed fine after I got stopped, but I was not about to take a chance on it again," she told him.

"Absolutely not! You did the right thing, Jill. They're looking at it now are they?"

"Yes, I could see they had it up on the hoist before I came upstairs to the waiting area. I should know something pretty fast and then how long it'll take to fix it. So unless you hear from me to the contrary, I think you'd better swing by and pick me up because I'll need a drive home."

"Sure, I'm going to get out of here in the next couple of hours or so. You should know what's going on by then. So call me and give me a heads up."

She ended the call and was halfway through an outdated magazine some time later when she heard her name paged over the PA system to come to the service desk.

Tom the service manager was waiting to speak to her. "Mrs. Sayer we couldn't find anything wrong with your car. We ran the usual tests on the computer's acceleration system and it could not detect a problem. In other words it did what it was supposed to do. I even took it up to the highway myself for a test drive and I could find absolutely nothing wrong. And as for the battery, we checked that too and it's a good battery. I can't imagine why it went dead. Was your door was left ajar or something? That could do it."

"Well no because I had to unlock my car to get in, but I'm more bothered by how it managed to accelerate on its own. It was very frightening."

He regarded her sympathetically. "I'm sorry, I have no explanation for that. All we can do is test the car to see where the computer malfunction is and nothing showed up. I don't know what else to say to you, other than to drive it and see if it happens again. If it does, don't panic. Press hard on the brake pedal with both feet to slow the vehicle, and shift into neutral. By shifting the transmission into neutral it will disengage the power to the wheels, and then find a safe place to stop."

She told him about her attempt to stop it with the brakes, but even that wouldn't work.

He spread his hands. "Then I'm at a loss too because we also checked the braking system and it's fine. I seriously do not have an explanation for what happened, but if you notice anything wrong, anything at all, bring it back here immediately on the back of a tow truck. Do not try to drive it."

Tamping down her frustration, she thanked him and called Brody again to relay the latest turn of events. The car performed perfectly on the drive home. She also acknowledged with chagrin that when she didn't get back to the constable with a note from the mechanic, he'd think she'd been lying to him and that nettled her.

* * *

The next day she started out for Charlottetown with understandable trepidation, but the drive in was blessedly uneventful. She drove under the speed limit and probably would for the rest of her life. She would never forget the terror of being in what felt like an out of control rocket.

Her meeting with Jack was productive and he liked the direction she was going with the play. She already felt good about how it was shaping up, but when a director of Jack's caliber gave you a thumbs up it was a great feeling of validation.

She was surprised when Brody walked into the kitchen at 3:00 p.m. wearing a downcast expression. What now!

"What's wrong, Brody?" she asked him after he sank into a chair at the kitchen table. "Or dare I ask?"

Closing his eyes momentarily, he sighed deeply. "I lost my job, babe. Don Sommers called me in after lunch and told me I was all through. Apparently it was a unanimous decision by the partners. I feel as if I've been poleaxed."

Jill was stunned. "But why? You work really hard and you were part of the negotiating team that helped land that big account. What on earth went wrong?"

"Amanda. That's what went wrong. I'm not surprised she'd be vindictive because I know it was her who orchestrated my dismissal. You see, her grandfather is filthy rich and when Don hired her she brought his investment portfolio with her. That was a huge shot in the arm for the firm. In any case, she didn't get what she wanted with me so she went to dear old granddad and he threatened to withdraw his business. Payback. It was an economic decision and it didn't help that Sommers also wanted me gone."

"But you can sue them for wrongful dismissal and you'd win."

"If it ended up going to court that whole business with Amanda could come out and that would be more damaging than a lost job. The lawyer's fees alone would kill me. Besides, they were very generous because they knew I did have a good case against them, so I have as much or more than I would have gotten in a lawsuit. I'll triple that in no time with smart investments."

"You don't want your job back?"

"You know, I knew Don was gunning for me and I basically played right into his hands with the Amanda thing. So I blame myself. I was ready to fight Sommers to the wall if he made a move against me, but I decided on the way home that I don't want my old job back. I've been dissatisfied with working there for a long time, and I'm mad at myself for not leaving on my own, for giving him the chance to fire me. But I'll come out of this a better man. I'll shop around. I've got a solid track record in the industry and a good resume. I'm going to give myself a few days to unwind from all of this and then I'll hit the bricks. Think you can stand to have me underfoot for a few days?"

She knelt by the chair and put her arms around his neck. "I'm going to love having you around. I love you, Brody."

* * *

The ghost tour for Yeo House was set to begin at 4:30 that afternoon. She'd been a little disappointed it wouldn't be held after dark, but realized that as participants were permitted to go beyond the rope barriers during the tour, it would be unsafe to do so in darkness. Besides, the entire thing would only take an hour and a half.

On this particular occasion there were just a handful of ghost hunters present and she had to give full kudos to the facilitator. She had the whole spooky thing down pat, which lent an appropriate sense of apprehension to the event.

Slowly the group made its way through the mansion, keen anticipation on the faces of those present, including her own she had to admit. She supposed she could be proven wrong, although she doubted it.

She recalled the TV news story about the group of dedicated ghost hunters who had recently visited the Yeo premises and determined there was indeed paranormal activity in the house. And they were seasoned pros. But could someone who believed in such things find what they were looking for? Detect something to indicate a presence so as not to lose face? Those were valid questions.

Jill also knew that those who believed in spirits also believed they could communicate through the manipulation of energy, hence the flashlight. Referred to as flashlight communication, she'd read where if there actually was a presence, they would respond to yes or no questions by flicking the light off or on. She'd read about that too. The goal was dialogue with a paranormal entity, and apparently there were flashlights designed specifically for paranormal investigation. That was going quite a stretch as far as she was concerned. How easy would it be to rig something like that, although she tried to keep an open mind and did not want to be unfair to those who took this type of work seriously.

Regardless, she was enjoying the air of anticipation within the group, or most of them. And then she heard it — they all did. An audible gasp. It seemed to come from behind, but when they wheeled around there was no one there. Jill had half expected to see another guest behind her and thus the sharp inhale would be easily explained, but it was Jill herself at the back of the group. This was all good stuff, but the whole ghost thing was beginning to wear thin. After she finished writing the play and it was staged, she did not plan to return to Yeo House.

Ever. Whether or not there was anything unusual going on here, she had satisfied any curiosity she had about the place. And she never wanted to see Wheelie again.

The group waited quietly to see if the sound would be repeated. It was not.

"Do you think it's angry?" one wide-eyed woman wanted to know. "Are we in danger?"

The woman's husband held her hand in a white-knuckled grip, either because he was more afraid than his wife, or he was duty-bound to protect her from whatever might come flying out of the woodwork. It helped to see the humour in all of this, although that *had* been a legitimate gasp. She'd clearly heard it herself and it had given her goosebumps, but clearly they were not in any danger.

And then as they all stood waiting for the tour to continue, a door upstairs closed with a thud. Not a house-shaking thud, but a definitive sound all the same. The nervous woman shrieked, which proved to be unsettling. If someone was that easily frightened, this was not for them. From all previous accounts, it was nothing out of the ordinary for the mansion.

Right, thought Jill but managed to keep the sardonic smile off her face. Was the whole thing staged? No, she knew the staff would have more integrity than to do such a thing. Maybe set something up for Halloween where people expected ... craved things that went bump in the night, but this was tame by comparison. Whatever accounted for this phenomenon, it was believed to be real and she was pleased to be given the opportunity to share it.

The shadows in the house were beginning to lengthen as the group reached the bottom of the stairs that led to the second floor. The husband of the fraidy cat woman now had his arm looped securely around her waist as they hesitated. Then, apparently resigning themselves to their fate, fell into place behind the others. Jill could not explain why she felt such trepidation. She'd been force-feeding herself this stuff for so long had she started to believe it? No. She did not. So still at the rear of the group, she climbed the stairs.

Naturally the first room everyone wanted to see was where Wheelie was kept. There was no mistaking he was the star of the show as everyone crowded around his plexiglass enclosure. One thing was for certain, Jill thought, he hadn't gotten any better looking since she'd been here last.

"He's so cute!" said another woman amid a chorus of "Awwws!"

He might have been cute at one time, Jill reasoned to herself, the only member of the small group not to vocalize her adoration for the toy. It was comical how people went crazy about something found in a wall, but wouldn't take a second look at anything from modern-day cleanup. It was not an uncommon experience to find discarded items when renovating old houses. She remembered one woman telling her that when she was a girl during the 1930's, people put their trash out on the river ice prior to spring break up. When the ice eventually melted, presto! Everything was gone.

When she'd asked the woman where she thought the junk had gone, the woman had simply replied: "I don't know, away I guess."

Out of sight out of mind like Brody said, and so anything that needed to be gotten rid of back then was also hidden in walls, in lieu of ice she thought to herself. Great solution seeing as how it stayed where it was for well over a hundred years. Others said the practice was to bring a home's inhabitants good luck, and still others said it was meant to serve as insulation.

A teenager ahead of her looked back at Jill. "Isn't he adorable?" she cooed while studying Wheelie. "I could take him right home with me."

Jill smiled politely. "It looks as though he's been played with a lot. I'd say he was a favourite toy."

The teenager sighed dreamily "Wouldn't it be nice to be able to go back and live in those times," she said wistfully. "Things would have been so much better."

Jill smiled and nodded. True there were some things that made one wish they could go back in time, but it was easy to come up with a list of plausible reasons why it would be a terrible idea. She would leave the girl to her whimsy.

Being tall had its advantages and Jill easily saw over the heads of the people in front of her. She looked at Wheelie and darned if that thing wasn't glaring straight at her. He couldn't be, so why did it seem so? Two black glass eyes couldn't just come to life. She shivered. Yes, she'd be very glad when this whole thing was over.

Another woman in the group, the one with a southern accent, leaned in for a closer look at Wheelie. "I read where this toy is supposed to be haunted. What makes you think so?"

The guide smiled as she recounted the Wheelie story.

The woman was also clearly a skeptic, and Jill's ears perked up. "How do you know someone wasn't moving it around, you know, having fun," the guest suggested. "Isn't that entirely possible?"

The guide, likely having dealt with her fair share of naysayers, explained the locking up and alarm setting procedure.

The woman shook her head. "I think someone is toying with you, excuse the pun. I'm sure there is a perfectly logical explanation."

The guide never missed a beat, listening patiently while the woman offered what she believed to be the true version of events. However everyone, except Jill, soon drowned her out in favour of their own beliefs. They were having a good time, and this woman was raining on their parade. She remained silent throughout the remainder of the tour.

As promised the tour ended at six o'clock, and Jill thanked the guide for an entertaining event and headed for her car. It felt good to get back out into the fresh air.

She'd told Brody she planned to stop for a few groceries and ran into Paula at the supermarket. They decided to go for a quick cup of coffee before they started to shop. Jill called Brody and told him not to expect her before dark, and he said to take her time. He had some yard work to do and planned to relax with a cold drink in the gazebo afterward, then turn in early.

As expected it was coming dark when she pulled into the driveway, and awww, there was Brody watching for her from the living room window. He was likely making sure she was okay after the experience she'd had with her car. A lamp burned softly in the background, throwing Brody into deep shadow. Grabbing a bag of groceries she started for the front door instead of going around to the back. She was about to open the door when the figure in the window moved. My lord! It was not Brody!

Chapter 16

She had the door open by the time she realized it was Bear Boy who'd been watching her from the shadows.

"Brody!" she shouted, fumbling with the light switch in the entrance to no avail. The bulb must have burned out. Even by lamplight she could see there was no one in the window, the living room empty. Her mind was playing tricks on her.

She called for Brody again. No answer.

Going into the kitchen she set the bag of groceries on the counter. And then she remembered guiltily that he said he was going to turn in early and here she was shouting.

"Oops," she whispered to herself. "Sorry."

Going to the bedroom door she was about to pull it closed, but on second thought stepped into the room to see if he was in bed. Tiptoeing closer she could see the bed was empty. Oh! That was a surprise! Where was he? If he was in the house, why hadn't he answered her? Was he even home at all, or had he left with someone. Doubt began to sneak back in, but she shoved it away. No, she wasn't going to go down that path again.

Starting out of the bedroom she got no further than the door. It wouldn't open. Making sure it was unlocked she tried again, but as hard as she pulled it would not budge. It had never stuck like this before. She'd have Brody take a look at it tomorrow. The lock must have jammed or something. Carefully she locked the door then unlocked it again and it opened easily. She'd make sure not to close it in case the same thing happened again. On the heels of that she recalled that she hadn't closed it behind her when she'd come in. Yet it was closed when she went to leave. Crazy!

No matter, there were groceries in the car that needed to get put away, especially the ice cream. Not a good idea to leave ice cream in the car in August if you didn't want a melted mess. So out she went and grabbed the last two bags, locking the car behind her. She was starting into the house when she saw the same shadowy figure appear in the window. What on earth was causing it! She stopped in her tracks and studied the indistinct spectacle. She yelped when the face came closer to the window. It was Bear Boy for sure, but how could it be him when he was at her mother and father's house, miles away. And he'd gotten so tall!

Squaring her shoulders she opened the door and marched into the house straight into the living room. Despite the shadows cast by the glow of the single lamp she could easily see the room was empty. Going to the kitchen she set the bags on the counter and returned to the living room, crossing over to the bay window. Was Brody playing a practical joke? There was nothing in the window or in the living room that even remotely resembled that horrible teddy bear. In fact she didn't see anything at all out of the ordinary.

She busied herself over the next few minutes putting groceries away and once finished went looking through the house for her husband, but Brody was not to be found. The baffling part was having to do most of it in the dark. For whatever reason the lights in some rooms worked, while others seemed to be burned out. And the feeling that she was being watched was completely unnerving. Who or what could be watching her? She didn't see anyone. Surely there wasn't a peeping Tom in the neighbourhood, but she couldn't shake the feeling. Her heart skidded to a stop momentarily. Was that someone breathing?

"Brody!" she called loudly. "Where are you?"

She felt a little silly shouting to an empty house, but she was growing more uneasy by the moment. Surely if he had gone out he would have let her know, but then she'd come home a little earlier than expected. Had he thought he'd make it home before she did? If so, why hadn't he taken his own vehicle? There had to be a note she'd missed in the kitchen because that's where he'd leave it knowing she'd be putting groceries away.

She searched the kitchen thoroughly but could not find a note. She tried the hall light again before going into the living room, and her heart leapt into her throat when she saw that same shadowy figure sitting in Brody's recliner rocking back and forth, back and forth.

"Brody?" she asked, knowing Brody never rocked in the chair. The sound of her own voice frightened her.

She stood, frozen to the spot, not taking her eyes off the recliner. The shadow moved and she clearly saw the outline of ears on either side of a large round head. How did that bear get into this house! She backed up slowly, her heart pounding. The teddy bear climbed down off the chair slowly, menacingly, his glossy black eyes fixed on her. A scream tore from her throat as hands came around her from behind.

"Why are you standing here practically in the dark?" Brody asked. "Jill, you're shaking like a leaf. What's wrong, honey? Are you okay?"

She turned and sank weakly against him. "I'm fine, but where were you and why were you trying to scare me? Why would you do such a thing, Brody?"

"Trying to scare you! I wasn't trying to scare you. I fell asleep out in the gazebo and came in the back door. Didn't you hear me?"

She hadn't. She'd been too focused on what she thought she'd seen in the living room. "No, I was busy putting the groceries away and then I thought I saw something in here. It was creepy and when you wouldn't answer me I thought you were playing a prank on me."

"Now, Jill, when have you ever known me to play a prank on anyone. I'm not the prank playing type and I did tell you when I was talking to you earlier that I was going to relax in the gazebo."

He was right, he had, and she'd forgotten. For some reason that ghost tour had set her on edge. She might not believe in any of it, but she had a vivid imagination and it was carrying her away to someplace awful. Someplace she didn't want to be.

"Why didn't you turn on the light instead of standing here in the dark? The one in the back hall doesn't seem to be working, but this one should be," he said starting for the switch to turn on the light behind them.

Suddenly every light in the house came on and burned brighter than the bulb wattage capacity. They shone with the intensity of a searchlight. Absolutely blinding. And then in a heartbeat the lights returned to their normal volume.

Brody looked dumbstruck. "What was that!"

Jill was equally shocked. "I didn't know normal lights could get that bright."

Brody was still gazing around in disbelief. "They can't. I could feel the heat! I'm calling an electrician first thing tomorrow to come and check out the wiring in this place. It should be up to code, but I don't want to take any chances. That was unreal."

Jill nodded her head vigorously. "Something's going on with this house, Brody. I have no clue what it might be, but I tell you I saw that awful teddy bear in the window when I was coming in the front door earlier – twice I saw him watching me."

Brody regarded her with a surprised chuckle. "Now that I don't believe. Sorry," he added holding up his hands in mock defense. "Didn't you say your mother and father came to pick that bear up for Della? The lights I believe, babe, because I saw it with my own eyes, but being stalked by a teddy bear is too ... out there." He laughed as if to soften the mood. "I think you've been hanging out at the Yeo place too much. You've been converted into a believer."

She was sorry she'd brought it up, but now she had, "Brody, I am a rational adult and I know what I saw. That thing was looking out the front window at me. If I'd thought quickly enough I'd have whipped out my phone and gotten a picture of it. Next time I will."

Brody threw up his hands. "Okay, Jill, you saw the teddy bear."

"Well I did."

He smiled. "Okay, so where did it go? Just disappear into thin air?"

She folded her arms, also smiling. "Okay, smart guy. Mum and Dad don't go to bed until midnight, after they've watched their favourite late show. I'm going to call them and see if *Bear Boy* is still there."

"Call them now? Nah, you'll scare them half to death. They'll think something's wrong. Besides, if it was at their place, how did it get back here? Fly? Grab a taxi?"

"They could have dropped him off when we weren't home."

"Does he have his own key?"

"Very funny, but when they say no, he's not there, I'm going to expect an apology. And don't worry about the time. I've called late before. Mum will answer because the phone's right beside her chair."

Her mother answered and Jill immediately assured her there was nothing wrong, she just had a quick question.

"Go ahead, dear. What was it you wanted to know?"

"I'm sure you recall that beat-up old teddy bear that Dad came to get for Della. Did you bring it back here, or is it still at your house?"

Celia Donovan groaned. "It's still here, I'm afraid. As a matter of fact Della's sleeping with it. I tell you, Jill, sometimes I wonder if that thing knows what we're saying. When it looks at me those eyes of his feel so real. I swear they track me."

Thanking her mother Jill finished the conversation, feeling worse than she had before she'd placed the call. "It's still at their house," she said miserably. "Mum thinks it's creepy too."

Brody sat down beside her on the sofa. "I agree with the creepy part, but Della likes him so we're going to have to put up with it. Now I'm not going to rub salt in the wound, but I for one will be glad when you finish the play about the paranormal. I think all this stuff is starting to get to you. I'm serious."

She sighed wearily. "You could be right, but I've never known my eyes to play tricks on me before. I'm not asleep when I'm seeing this stuff. I'm wide awake." She didn't mention that her dreams were filled with the same things.

Brody reached up and undid the clip that held her hair in place. Long golden curls tumbled over his hand. "I know a good way to get your mind off all that woo woo stuff," he said as he leaned in for a kiss. It quickly gained momentum as she kissed him back with equal intensity.

Still kissing her he pulled her to her feet. Scooping her up in strong arms he started for the bedroom, but when he got there the door wouldn't open. He reluctantly set her down on her feet while he fought with the door, but it refused to budge. Jill giggled as he picked her up again and went down the hall to the spare room where they temporarily forgot about the stressors of the past few days.

Later as they lay there suffused in afterglow, Brody fell asleep and Jill reflected. She couldn't help but think about the unusual events she had been experiencing. She had obviously angered entities unknown, because although she was loathe to admit it, she now acknowledged that not everything could be neatly explained away. As pragmatic as she was, she could not ignore the sights and sounds that had been visited upon her. Okay, she said, mentally raising the white flag of surrender, I believe. You got me, now back off and leave me alone.

Six Months Later

Jack was thrilled with the completed script and casting went very well.

Of course there were changes to be made, welcome suggestions from the actors who were tasked with the job of bringing the playwright's characters to life. The coveted part of Wheelie went to a veteran actor, small enough of stature that he'd make the toy believable. They'd pared the number of actors down to six, including two ghostly figures and an extra or two. That was their limit for the rather modest-sized stage. What the playhouse lacked in stage size however, they more than made up for with a pleasingly intimate theatre experience. Jill had decided that each of the actors would also serve as narrators throughout the piece, a suggestion that Jack enthusiastically supported.

The set designer had his work cut out for him to bring this production to life, but the results proved to be stellar. To Jill's relief, the players themselves couldn't contain their laughter at times and in all the right places. When interviewed by an arts columnist for a tease about her upcoming play, she characterized it as simply another way to look at the paranormal. She also made a point to salute the friendliness and professionalism of staff members at all of the sites she'd visited throughout Prince Edward Island, and that she meant no disrespect.

As opening night approached, Jill dealt with the usual butterflies. What if nobody laughed? What if only the players, the director and she herself found it funny? What if people walked out ... thought her play was a total bomb? She reminded herself yet again that she'd been through all this before and would make it through this one too. It wasn't easy to make herself so vulnerable. Even if there were detractors, controversy was good for sales, always had been, always would be. Jack had convinced her it was going to be a hit, but one never knew until they'd tested the mood of an audience.

It was a tightrope walk at best. Sometimes if you assured people they'd get a big laugh out of something, expectations ran too high and their reaction didn't match the hype. Jill found it agonizing to sit through the first act of any of her plays. People usually didn't laugh much at the beginning because they were still trying to grasp the gist of the story and get to know the characters. The big laughs usually came in the last act, after the second act warmed them up a little more. And then there was the intermission before the third act when wine was available. People seemed ready to laugh after a glass of wine. Great! Bring it on.

As opening night approached and all was in readiness for their January debut, a severe weather system moved into the Maritimes. Stalling overhead, it dumped a foot of snow on most of the Island. It was a good old-fashioned blizzard, snowing for the best part of three days creating hazardous conditions. The wind howling like a banshee knocked down power lines that threw the province into the dark. When the storm finally abated and serious cleanup got underway, power outages continued to plague the area leaving tens of thousands without hydro.

And most tragically of all, one of the lead players experienced a heart attack while shovelling his driveway. The playhouse itself suffered significant damage with the partial collapse of its roof from ice and snow load. It was ludicrous to think the play could go ahead for the foreseeable future, and none were more disappointed than the director and the playwright herself. Endless hours had already been spent preparing for the week-long run, and now everyone involved would be cooling their heels until at least spring, or possibly even summer.

"If there's one bit of good news in all of this," Jack mused as he stirred his coffee a week later, "it's that Henry survived his heart attack and is recovering nicely. He's already undergone surgery and since we won't be proceeding for the next few months, I'm happy to say he's still going to be able to perform."

Jill sighed. "We're all so thankful that Henry is going to be okay. I know this sounds crazy, but that storm seemed to come out of nowhere. I checked the weather for opening night, as I'm sure you did too, and it was supposed to be sunny and cold for a week. Next thing you know *that* happened."

"I agree it sounds crazy but winter happens, kiddo. This isn't the first opening night that's bombed. I once was directing a play when the male lead and his understudy both came down with a severe case of food poisoning. They'd had supper together and got some bad seafood. They had to be hospitalized. The play was the last thing on their minds."

Jill wrinkled her brow. "That *is* rough."

"It's every director's nightmare," said Jack. "I say a prayer for the safety and wellbeing of the cast – for all the right reasons. But then there's fate and we're all at the mercy of that."

"Such is live theatre I guess," she said. "Onward and upward."

* * *

Jill took a much-needed break over the next few months, recovering from a tumultuous late summer and fall. She and Della spent a lot of time outdoors and with a snowy winter underway, Della had ample opportunity to perfect her snow angels.

And Jill and Brody had never been closer. He'd had no trouble finding work in a large financial institution and they planned a trip away together in March. Brody had made their vacation a condition of employment and management was so pleased to acquire this bright young financial advisor they were only too happy to agree. Two weeks in Jamaica was just what they needed to fall in love all over again, and they returned starry-eyed.

The best news of all was the grant Jack was able to secure for a new roof for the playhouse, and construction was slated to get underway the second week in April.

"Can I go to your play, Mommy?" Della asked one day after Jill picked her up from preschool.

Jill was at the counter making a snack for her daughter. "No, sweetie, not yet. We have to wait until you're a little older."

"Next week?"

Jill laughed. "No, it'll be a little longer than that, but don't worry. When you're old

271

enough you can go with Mommy and Daddy and it'll be fun. This time you're going to stay with Grandma and Grandpa for the week the play is running. They'll take you to preschool and pick you up. Doesn't that sound like fun?"

She agreed that it was, already looking forward to the visit that would take place at the end of May.

And then it was opening night all over again, the butterflies that had been lying dormant since January reignited in a lively dance in her midsection. All was in readiness, and as if to make up for her lack of good manners during the winter, Mother Nature bestowed upon them an idyllic balmy Prince Edward Island evening. To a person every theatre goer had retained their ticket, so they were promised a full house once again.

Even better was that Henry had made a complete recovery from his heart attack and subsequent surgery. He was in the pink of health and now fully committed to a healthier lifestyle. The cast quickly slipped back into their characters.

However, Michelle, who was playing the mother, tested positive for COVID hours before show time and was feeling too sick to go on. She did not have an understudy, so Jack called on a young actress who wasn't the best but having no alternative on such short notice, he'd taken her on.

When the curtain rose on the first act, Brody squeezed Jill's hand encouragingly. She knew he understood she was on pins and needles, hardly daring to breathe. But they were here and so far, in the first five minutes at least, all was going smoothly. And then the power went out, throwing the stage into complete darkness. There were gasps and mumblings among the audience now sitting in the dark, without even the subdued lighting of wall sconces. Jill was sure her heart was beginning to miss some very important beats. She could see theatre staff hurrying about with flashlights, obviously trying to identify the problem and get it fixed. And then as quickly as it had disappeared, the electricity returned, the stage lights back on, catching the players unaware — much to the amusement of the audience. It did look pretty funny.

And so the play proceeded and after the lights had been on for a while, it seemed all would continue to go smoothly. Until the actress who replaced Michelle came onstage, tripped over her own feet and was sent sprawling just short of the footlights. For some reason she found that gaffe amusing and began to laugh. Jill wanted to strangle her and Jack would be apoplectic, but the audience thought it was hysterical.

Onward it went, and then Henry for some inexplicable reason completely forgot his lines. You could hear the prompter's loud whisper as he stared to the side of the stage seeking her help. He apparently couldn't hear her and to Jill's horror he turned to the audience with a wide grin and shrugged with arms outstretched and palms up in surrender. The crowd ate it up.

When Wheelie was re-enacted, promising to be a show-stopper, the motorized wheeled framework he was squatting on, on all fours, failed. So they tried to push him onstage and one wheel fell off, just like the real thing. The actor had all he could do to maintain his balance. It was one amusing mishap after another.

Jill could hear Brody laughing beside her, his hand over his mouth to hide it from her, but soon she was laughing too. And the audience laughed loudly as the cast continued to limp through the production.

There also seemed to be some woo woo stuff going on, although she knew Jack would never admit to those added details. No one could explain the figure draped in white that seemed to float across the stage and frighten poor Henry out of his wits. Not great for a man with a history of heart issues. And the loud crash of thunder that shook the theatre and caused squeals of surprise from frightened audience members. Odd that there was no rain or lightning.

And then it was over, blessedly.

A newspaper reporter was waiting in the lobby to speak to Jill. "How does it feel to have another hit play?" he wanted to know. "The special effects were fantastic! The lights going out was the perfect touch. I watched the entire thing. It was a riot!"

"Thank you so much," Jill told him. "There's usually a few bugs on opening night, but I'm so glad you enjoyed the production."

Any ink the play received was positive, and Jill breathed an enormous sigh of relief. She'd spoken to Jack briefly after the curtain call, and he claimed to be as bewildered as she was that practically everything had gone wrong. Even the blackout at the beginning of the play remained a mystery.

The rest of the week was as eventful as opening night had been. Jack and Jill had stopped trying to explain some of the more unusual incidents and simply held on for the ride.

Jill received a lot of interest in her play, still intrigued by the special effects.

* * *

As darkness settled over the Yeo mansion, the doors long since locked and alarms activated to discourage any unauthorized visitors, the old building breathed an audible sigh of contentment. Wheelie looked around the small bedroom, waiting patiently to be lifted from his daytime plexiglass prison and taken on his nightly adventure. What fun they had together. But they had to be mindful of approaching daylight when the little toy dog

275

would once again be put back in place, and his playmate hiding until darkness returned.

Wheelie heard the heavy footsteps as they made their way slowly up the carpeted stairway. His heart was alive with eager anticipation. And then there it was, that sweet happy face peering around the doorframe in a game as old as the house itself. Bear Boy was such a trickster.

Epilogue

Brody Sayer loved his new job and went home every night, a happy man.

Don Sommers left his wife and married Amanda Leland. It was not a match made in heaven.

Jill Sayer's play Ghosts in the House? was a smash hit wherever it played.

Della Sayer remained inseparable from Miss Ezzy. She never mentioned Punch Willigan or Bear Boy ever again. The teddy bear had simply vanished from their lives. Not long after he left, a plush purple octopus with pink hair was delivered to the Sayer residence. The little girl welcomed it with open arms.

One year later Jill, Brody and Della moved into their dream home overlooking the beautiful Northumberland Strait. As the moving van pulled away Jill would not even look back at their former house on Mayflower Lane. Unseen eyes in the attic watched them leave.

The End

Eden Monroe loves giving voice to the endless parade of interesting characters who introduce themselves in her imagination. She writes about real life, real issues and struggles, and triumphing against all odds. A proud east coast Canadian, she enjoys a variety of outdoor activities and a good book.

She is at:

https://www.bookswelove.com/shop?tag=Eden%20Monroe

Please visit her webpage: https://edenmonroeauthor.com

You can find her on Facebook at: facebook.com/AuthorEdenMonroe/

Eden Monroe books also published by BWL Publishing

Dare To Inherit
Gold Digger Among Us
When Fate Comes Calling (Book One Emerald Valley Ranch series)
Storms in the Valley (Book Two Emerald Valley Ranch series)
Back in the Valley (Book Three Emerald Valley Ranch series)
Incomplete Truths (Book Four Emerald Valley Ranch series)
Unforeseen Shadows (Book Five Emerald Valley Ranch series)
Just Before Sunset
Almost Broken
Sidelined
Looking for Snowflakes
Dangerous Getaway
Sudden Turn (Book One The Martel Sisters trilogy)
Barlowe Pride (Book Two The Martel Sisters trilogy)
Sunrise Interrupted (Book Three The Martel Sisters trilogy)
Who Buried Sarah (Canadian Historical Mysteries – New Brunswick)

Bound for Somewhere (Book One The Kavenaghs trilogy)

When Shadows Stir (Book Two The Kavenaghs trilogy)

BWL Publishing

bwlpublishing.ca